Festival of Time:
Book Two:
Rescue

To Nina,

Happy reading...

Festival of Time:
Book Two:
Rescue

By C.L. Peache

Clpeache

Clparke

Festival of Time: Book Two: Rescue

ISBN: 9798797626725

Copyright © C.L. Peache 2022

Independently published, available in paperback or e-book.

First published 2022

Cover design by Christine Goldschmidt

Typesetting by The Book Typesetters
thebooktypesetters.com
us@thebooktypesetters.com
07422 598 168

Acknowledgements

Special thanks to everyone who has helped with the
publication of this book and the moral support needed
to create this piece of fiction and
in no particular order, special thank go to...

Maria, Bonnie, Ric, my family, Sandra, The Derby,
Newark and Fosseway Crew.

Thank you to my Facebook friends who chose some of
the dragon names.

Christine Goldschmidt for the stunning cover.

Rachael and Nat at The Book Typesetters for the
stunning typesetting – love the dragons!

Prologue...

Ruler of all dragons, King Pathanclaw and his grandson Pathandon emerged through the portal. Pathanclaw carried Prince Villian, future ruler of Arcus. Their mission was to reunite dragons and humans and finally return to their home world of Arcus to rescue the world from the Masters army which was ready to attack.

Thanan astride Pathandon with Pol clinging tightly behind him; Star proudly riding her Dragon with an unwanted guest in the form of Triana at her back. The friends had escaped the Masters on Luminosa, a place they had been held from a young age, forced to do the Masters' bidding and learn the art of magic. Now they were returning to save the children left behind and the dragons who had been stolen thousands of years ago...

The Children – Luminosa

Kyla had calculated her age wrong; she must have. As she came out of the cave, a Master was waiting for her. She knew what this meant. She looked around, wide-eyed, searching for help, but there was no-one to rescue her. She bowed her head, acknowledging her fate. She hoped Galan would carry on with their plan. The Masters had to be stopped when the time came. They all knew it now. They had to be stopped.

She thought about using her magic. She could get away into the forest, but she'd felt her memories return as she travelled through the cave and had felt her magic wain as she emerged out of the darkness. The Suckers had done their job. As if she, just a girl, had any chance against the Masters anyway. Why had she deluded herself into believing she would return, that one day, she would get back home to the rolling fields and the farm she loved? At least she had her memories. Her mother, father and brothers would be waiting for her. They would welcome her home, and she would show them her magic tricks. Unlike others, she had remembered her past, and she could die knowing her past was real. It was more than the other children.

Kyla fell in step behind the Master and studied her adversary. What were they under the black hooded cloaks? People, just like her. Maybe if she attacked him from behind, she could hold him down, and the other children could help. But she knew it was only a fantasy; she knew it wouldn't help. The Masters had recently dealt a new punishment; they would inflict their displeasure on your closest friends. If you didn't have any friends, the Masters would punish all the children. It only served to increase the divide between her friends.' Kyla thought this had been used to dispel any thoughts of rebellion once the Star, Thanan, Pol, and Triana had left during the Festival of Time. The Masters had laughed. The children left behind had been shocked and silent, expecting repercussions for creating spells and letting their creatures run amok.

Kyla and Galan had spoken about it late into the evening. There had been so much excitement during the Festival of Time. After the group had disappeared, the magic hadn't been taken away from the children as they feared. It was like they'd been given a gift, and they made full use of it. Kyla wondered why Triana had left with the others. She was arch enemies with Star and Thanan. Kyla had hated following in Triana's wake, but she tried to take a step back when it came to bullying the other children. She knew Triana carried favour with the Masters and had hoped being close to her would help her escape one day.

Kyla tried to take in everything as they left the cave. When she thought back, maybe her worm, she'd decided never to name it like some of the others – it just made it harder when you had to say goodbye, maybe her worm had been saying goodbye, and she'd not even realised. How could they know it was time for the children to go? So many questions, always so many questions. She wondered if adults had so many or if they were blessed with the answers.

The solid stone floor soon gave way to familiar mossy ground. The canopy of trees was so large it looked like it touched the skies. The purple sky was bright above them. Kyla noticed the Master walked through the flowery pathway without heed, whereas most of the children tried to avoid stepping on the flowers. She carefully stepped to one side to avoid a patch of bright red ones which always bloomed late in the day. Kyla grimaced as the Master twisted his boot as he walked through another patch of them flattening them into the ground. As Kyla turned back, she noticed they had sprung back up, tall and undamaged. It made her smile; if these simple flowers could deny the power of the Masters so could they. But was it too late?

"Where are you taking me?" She didn't expect an answer and was shocked when one was forthcoming.

"To the Suckers."

Kyla gasped. Why were they taking her there? No-one had ever seen them. Well, there were rumours that Star and Pol had come across them one day, but everyone decided it couldn't be true, because surely Star would have told them all. She wasn't one to keep things from them if they needed to know something. Star had tried to look after all of them.

Kyla had always felt sorry for Thanan and the way Triana treated him. Triana had once delighted in commenting on the fact that Kyla always blushed when around him. It had made Thanan's cheek redden as well, but it soon stopped when Star turned up. Triana hated challenging Star; she always came off the worst. Kyla envied Thanan and Star's friendship. She often watched them as they play fought in the camp. She didn't think they liked each other in that way; they were simply good friends. It was important to have friends here, but getting too attached, especially to the ones nearing thirteen, was hard.

"What's going to happen to me?" Kyla thought she might as well try again. Maybe the Master was in a good mood.

"Well, we are going to suck that magic right out of you. What else do you think a sucker is for?" Her blood ran cold. He was gleeful about it, as if something nice was going to happen to her.

"But, but what will happen to me?" Her voice trembled, and she clenched her fists, trying to be brave. If only Triana was here, maybe she would be able to help her. They were friends, after all.

"Who cares?"

Those two words made her heart break. Who cares? Her parents would care, her brothers would care, her friends would care, she cared. Her anger was starting to take over, a surge through her body. It wasn't fair. This couldn't be the way it ended. She had to do something, but what could she do without endangering the others?

As they emerged into the camp, her eyes scanned the children, looking for Galan; he needed to make sure he looked after the children. He came running from the direction of the training room, breathless. Their eyes met, their emotions reflected. They thought she had another year; it was too soon. The Masters always marched them through the camp to frighten the others into submission, but she held her head high as she took one last look at the place that had been her temporary home.

The huts required constant maintenance, it rarely rained on Luminosa and they spent a lot of time going to and fro to the river that flowed from the caves. They'd often wondered how the water kept running and presumed that wherever the water came from it rained a lot. On their free magic days, the children would make use of their magic or creatures to repair the huts or make new hammocks out of the giant leaves the trees shed. Once Pol had arrived, no-one dared chop anything down. One look from Pol and they'd stopped immediately. They'd found they could easy forage from the natural dead leaves.

Kyla followed the Master through the camp. The Master pointed at one of the other children, Kalen. He looked stricken. Kyla was sure he was only ten. Why were they taking him? She'd heard he wasn't doing well in the training camp, and his dragon or lizard creature hadn't materialised. It looked like the Masters were getting impatient. Kalen looked frantically around at the others, but there was nothing they could do. His shoulders reflected his acknowledgement of his fate, and he moved in step with Kyla. She reached out and took his hand.

She found Galan's eyes again, and they nodded at each other. He would try and make the children ready for the time when something happened, and they could fight back. One day they would. One day. This had to stop.

She found the walk through the woods strangely calming, it was a place she always loved to come when there was nothing else to do. The forest was quiet, but never silent even though no animals or birds inhabited this strange place. The soft moss created a comfortable bed. She would place her arms by her side, palms face down, close her eyes and let the forest talk to her.

Kyla would swear she could hear the trees talking to each other, their leaves rustling and branches creaking. She could hear the roots reaching deep into the ground, growing and expanding; the crackle of loss as one of the large leaves fell majestically to the floor to settle and await its fate; feeding the soil, fungus growing and providing new life. The flowers strained to reach up for the sky for sun and below for the water the trees provided. Forever stretching for life. There was a constant drip from the large lantern trees as the water nourished the ground throughout the day. She realised she would miss this place. Miss being at one with the forest.

"Come on."

The Master snarled at them, and their hands tightened, as they picked up the pace. They had been walking for hours and they were tired. Finally, after another hour, maybe more, the sky blackened. They arrived at the edge of the forest but the desolate dry land went on past their ability to see. The sight of the Suckers forced a gasp from them both. The sight of all those huge dragons took the children's breath away – the size of them. She counted them one by one. Twelve dragons. She could just see the vibrant colours which would have dazzled had the sand not covered them and the pitch black of the night not descended. She had never seen such a sight.

All the dragons turned their heads as one; they had great sorrow in their eyes. A tear trickled down Kyla's face unchecked. These dragons had seen such pain. Felt such pain. It broke her heart.

"Over here," The Master commanded.

There were torches lit in a circle in front of the dragons. She couldn't believe how big they were. Kyla had only just noticed the other men. Only normal men and not Masters; these were the first adults she had seen on Luminosa. They looked mean. She decided she preferred the cloaked Masters.

"Right, you. Come here," One of the men demanded of Kalen, whose hand tightened painfully around hers.

"Come on. Don't be such a baby. I've got work to do."

"It's okay, Kalen." She knew it wasn't, but what else could she say.

Kalen shuffled slowly towards the man, like whatever was going to happen. It might change if he walked just a little slower. He fell on his knees in front of the man and cried, "I will do better. I promise I will."

The man seemed indifferent. He grabbed Kalen's hand and clasped some iron restraints. Kyla could just see the iron ring the long chain was attached to. It didn't leave any room for him. Kalen was crying now and Kyla watched in horror as the man moved to one of the dragons and pulled out a large iron bolt which allowed the evil contraption over the dragon's mouth to open, just a little.

"What's happening?" she cried.

The Master sighed, "Always the same question. Can

you children not come up with something more imaginative after all these years?" He shook his head and said no more.

Kyla wanted to look away but couldn't. It was as if her eyes were fixed on two points; the dragon, the boy, the dragon, the boy. The Master raised his hand and a bolt of light shot from his finger and hit Kalen. He cried out more in surprise than pain, she thought. She could feel a rumbling from beneath the ground. The dragon was opening its mouth as the man poked it with something. A roaring in her ears and a blast of heat took her breath away. She dropped to the ground, her hands over her ears, her eyes tight shut. She didn't realise it had stopped, and kept screaming, until the Master kicked her.

As she slowly opened her eyes, she could barely bring herself to look. She heard a loud noise near the dragon; she presumed the bolt was being put back. Why didn't the dragon just burn the Master? Kyla watched as the Master moved the blackened sand around with his foot, staining the bottom of his cloak with Kalen's ashes. Looking with fresh eyes, Kyla could see many blackened patches on the sand. It made her feel sick. This is what happened when they turned thirteen. But why? Why just burn them? It didn't make any sense. Why make them train and learn magic and get creatures if they did this. She couldn't understand it.

The Master walked back to her. He was rolling something around in his hand, and as he came close, he stuck his hand out, and she saw two bright silver stones in his hands.

"Was hardly worth it for so little. These are not going to go far."

They were gems. Kyla wondered what they did with them, but her mouth had gone dry. Her tongue stuck to the roof of her mouth. She couldn't move. They were going to do this to her, right now, and she couldn't escape.

She couldn't even form magic. The connections were lost. Then she realised they must be blocked by the dragons. Or fear. She had never felt such fear.

"Come on then. Your turn."

The man was waiting in the blackened sand where Kalen had once been. Her legs were weak, and she wasn't sure she could move. The Master helped her along by pushing her as she tried to rise. She stumbled forward and dropped to the ground again. It wasn't fair; this wasn't how it should end. Surely this couldn't be it. She wished she could tell Galan to get the children and just run away or hide in the caves. Do something. Don't let this happen to any more children. How many had burnt over the years?

She felt a great pain in her body and turned to see the Master smiling at her. How could he perform magic when she could not? Her anger fuelled her, and she pushed her hand out and said the words. A tiny ball of fire shot out. The Master was as surprised as her, but he quickly held up his hand and muttered a few words. The fire died before it reached him.

"Interesting. This has never happened before. How did you manage to do that?"

"I, I don't know," she stammered. She didn't know. She didn't even really think about the words. The magic just came.

"I might need…" The Master cut his words short, as he seemed to be listening to another voice.

"Secure her," he shouted to the man. "It's time."

What was time? What had happened? The Master turned and walked back into the forest as the man grabbed her from behind and she felt the tight metal bonds dig into her wrists. He reached over and fixed a gag around her mouth, and digging a leg into her knee, he made her kneel. She felt sick as the puff of ashes covered her clothes. He then summoned some other men and they moved systematically down the line of dragons using whips, tightening the huge metal chains which forced the dragons to the ground.

Kyla looked ahead to the silver dragon that had burned her friend. She could see so much pain and sorrow, it made her heart break. It wasn't their fault she realised, and she tried to convey with her eyes that whatever they made the dragon do, she didn't blame them. The dragon moved its head ever so slightly. She felt it understood.

The men finished securing the dragons, as a crack sounded. It was as if the planet had split in two. Just like during the Festival of Time. Could this mean Triana had come back? Star? Thanan? Pol? Would one of them rescue her? Wouldn't they? She had to be ready. She tried to muster the anger she had felt earlier but fear was overtaking her again. She needed to clear the routes in her mind. As she delved further, she felt them opening one by one, as if she was running through a dense forest but the branches formed a clear path for her. The magic was forming, she looked at the silver dragon. It winked!

Chapter 1 – Luminosa

They were waiting for them.

Seven Masters, hooded, heads bowed, and the familiar feel of magic reached the company as they emerged through the portal. The power of magic that had been lost to Thanan, Star and Triana when they had left Luminosa, returned in a rush. They felt dizzy, as, once again, they felt the magic course through their bodies.

Three dragons and three riders faced the Masters. Time paused. The air crackled with anticipation. Who would make the first move? They hadn't expected the Masters to be waiting for them, their plans to rescue to the children and dragons already in doubt.

Thanan turned his head to the right and looked at Star astride Dragon. She looked every bit the warrior, her back straight and her long blue hair sticking up with the static of magic. Thanan felt his whole-body tingle as he felt the power surge back. Behind Star, he saw Triana smile. Triana was gripping the talisman that Pathanclaw, king of dragons, had quietly warned them about. Underneath him, Thanan felt Pathandon tense. The months of training had tuned Thanan into his friend's every movement when he had never thought in his wildest dreams he would be at one with a dragon. Thanan turned to his left to check on Villian – he was shouting something, but Thanan couldn't hear what it was. The silence as they faced the evil of the Masters was deafening, blood roared in his ears. Behind him, Pol gripped Thanan's body, their small fingers digging painfully into his sides.

Pathanclaw and Pathandon raised their giant heads as Thanan covered his face. He felt the heat of the flames as they directed their fury at the Masters before them. Thanan stared open-mouthed, surely this would be the end of them. Who could withstand the power of dragon flame? But the flames hit an invisible wall and danced over the dome-shaped protection shield the Masters had created. Amid this attack, Thanan realised Pathandon and Pathanclaw were shooting red flame and Dragon, blue flame. He stored away the question of whether all the dragons' flames represented their colour.

From the corner of his eye, Prince Villian spotted movement. Maybe forty or fifty children were circling the Masters as the flames stopped. Foolish! They would be burnt alive. Then he recognised the battle tactic. The Masters knew the dragons wouldn't burn innocent children when they thought freedom was near. He didn't have time to acknowledge the battle craft of these Masters before he turned, hearing Thanan cry out.

The children lined up outside the magical wall of protection. Some had their creatures with them, lizards, and dragons in front, protecting them. The magic users had their hands out, ready to cast whatever spell the Masters had ordered, although they didn't need the magic of these children, who were expendable, only there to protect the Masters from the magical powers of the dragons. One of the Masters raised his head and, very slowly, removed his hood, his hand gently letting go, as the hood rested down his back. His green eyes met the large red eyes of King Pathanclaw. Recognition flared in Pathanclaw's memory. Impossible. But deep down he had known it would come to this. Villian saw familiarity in his features.

A silence descended as Pathandon took in this black cloaked human. His grandfather's mind was open to him. He could hear disbelief but understanding. He could hear the questions running through the king's mind, trying to make sense of what he was seeing. Pathanclaw finally named him.

"*Barakar.*"

The human nodded, a slow smile creeping across his face. It was a face touched by youth which it should not have been. The gift of eternal life. This had only been given to a chosen few on Prince Villian and Pathanclaw's home planet of Arcus. The chosen ones, whom Pathanclaw trusted to see the world and time to this day. The gift of extended life was as much of a curse, as a gift. The time when 'the one' arrived and the worlds could return to their natural order, was upon them. But this? How had this come to pass? How had Barakar survived Arcus? But who else could have created the abomination on this planet? Pathanclaw knew it could only be one. Had known deep down if he'd been honest with himself. He should have let the knowledge be at the forefront of his decisions. Perhaps he would have chosen differently.

Pathandon felt his grandfather close his mind. Now was not the time. They were in greater danger than they'd imagined. They'd expected their arrival to be an unwelcome surprise and hoped to gain control of Luminosa quickly. Their aim had been to secure the Masters and free the children and the female dragons who were trapped on Suntra, but now it wasn't a clear path. Pathandon wondered who Barakar was. He turned his head in the direction Villian was already looking. He'd been surprised how quickly he'd got used to a human sitting on his back. It now felt strange without him.

Thanan turned again to Star. She and Dragon were ready to join the other dragons but behind her, Triana was holding the talisman. Triana's eyes were shut, whispering words of the magic which she now unleashed.

"Star, look out," Thanan cried.

Star turned to look at him, but too late. Thanan could

hear Pol in his mind chanting a spell, could feel the air move to make way for magic. The light moved around Star, Dragon and Triana. A protection spell. It had to be. As Thanan tried to turn to tell Pol to stop, Thanan, Prince Villian, Pol, Pathanclaw and Pathandon disappeared, leaving Star and Dragon to the fate of the Masters.

Chapter 2 – Suntra

The dragons gathered in the morning sun, their hearts heavy with the loss of General Battlewing. Bluewing stood close to his mother, who needed him now he was head of the family. His mother looked at her young son, trying to be brave and another piece of her heart splintered. How many more losses would they suffer before they were safe again? They had lost so many when they'd fled Arcus. So many mothers, fathers, sons, daughters, so much family. How much more could they bear?

Queen Silvarna's eyes were drawn to Kyanite and her son Bluewing. She closed her mind so the other dragons were sheltered from her thoughts. The day King Pathanclaw, her beloved had travelled through the Festival of Time portal with her grandson, Pathandon, she knew she might never see them again. She knew that could be the end of their journey, and for that split second, she felt happiness when she realised it was General Battlewing who had met his death and not her husband, not her grandson, but then she felt shame. Shame, that she, a queen, could set such a poor example by wishing the unhappiness of another to protect the ones who were hers. It was not queenly. It was not how a dragon behaved.

All dragons were family, they should not be more than the other. But Pathanclaw was her mate, her one true heart, and she'd always imagined they would end their lives together. Like their son, they would choose the time of their death. Even if her son made the ultimate sacrifice for his dying wife and knew he couldn't live without her. Still, it had been her hope, despite Pathanclaw embarking on the quest to find 'the one' who would help them return to Arcus and find the missing females. The line of dragons would fail if the females were lost forever. More family. More death. The end of the dragons. Could there ever be such a thing? Would the magic of the world allow it?

Queen Silvarna quietened the dragons. She was now the ruler until Pathanclaw returned. It was her responsibility to keep order and make sure that they were ready when her beloved returned for them. She hoped they would make the final journey back to their home of Arcus, to live in peace once again with the humans. They had to cling to this hope. She'd always trusted her mate and always would.

"Please, everyone, quieten your minds."

Gradually the dragons managed to still themselves, having learned at an early age to block out or shut off their minds to the collective.

"We all feel the loss of General Battlewing. Not only was he our general, a great dragon, who trained our group and worked towards making sure we survived. He was our friend, our family. We honour his death as we honour any of our number. We may not be able to honour them in our usual way. Sadly, there will be no long flight to the gem cave. But Battlewing will live on. He will live on in our memories and our hearts. His legacy will be our future. We will become strong. We will fight until we are back in our rightful place, living our peaceful life back on Arcus. We will make him proud."

Silvarna paused as the dragons roared their approval, the flames dancing in the air, shaking the very ground. Silvarna was proud to see the dragons acting as one. They would need this passion in the days, months, and years ahead. Her eyes sought out each dragon, to keep them in her memory and keep the family alive.

"I believe King Pathanclaw will have observed the old ways. General Battlewing's experience and magic will not have been wasted. His strength, power and wisdom will have graced our gems and will provide the magic we need to exist. It will live on in my grandson, Pathandon, as is our way."

Silvarna's eyes found Bluewing. What would he think about his best friend Pathandon receiving the powers from his father? They were best friends but fierce competitors. Would Bluewing be jealous? It was not a normal trait for a dragon but it could often be seen in the very young. Bluewing's eyes showed only pride. He was a true Blue dragon, a protector of the Royal Reds. He would defend them until his last breath of fire. She couldn't help but let her gratitude and emotion show to Bluewing. He bowed his head, showing so much promise, he would be bigger than his father. This loss would give him the passion and drive to succeed. She only hoped that it would not make him reckless. Only time would tell.

"Despite the sadness we all feel, we still have a duty. A duty to your King and General. They left orders and we will fulfil them. We will be ready when they return and we will fight to restore peace."

Silvarna knew that if Pathanclaw were here, he would tell her that she was always better at the speeches than he was. A king was nothing without his queen. The dragons on Suntra had been reduced by three, but she hoped, beyond hope, more of them would return and soon.

"General Bluewing. Please give me an update on how the younglings are progressing in their training. Your father gave you this great responsibility and we will make sure we are ready."

Bluewing looked up, wondering if he would ever get used to his new title. It came with both sadness and pride.

The ceremony had been strange due the absence of the King. The younglings had never known a new general to be sworn in. To humans, it would seem cruel and difficult to watch, but the General was the protector and had to be the strongest, the fastest, the best of them all. He had to have the respect of all the dragons if they were to follow him without question. Without a strong leader, the other dragons would be likely to assert their own dominance. But Bluewing was so young, he would be the youngest Blue ever to become a General. He wasn't sure he was ready, he needed more time with his father so he could acquire his vast amount knowledge and experience.

The night before the ceremony, Bluewing had flown for hours, across this world which was his home. The tales of Arcus made it feel like his, but Suntra was all he'd really known. Would Arcus feel the same? Would he feel an affinity with Arcus because it was his world? He hoped so. Tonight, was a night of reflection, to deem himself worthy. No-one would challenge him if he were confident he could be a worthy general. He thought of his father. It was easy to conjure him in his mind. He knew what his father would say. He was a Blue, a protector. It was their role, a royal without a Blue beside them was unthinkable. Bluewing would be the one. He would be ready when King Pathanclaw and his friend Pathandon returned. He would push the younglings harder. He could feel time slipping away, a rare and uncomfortable feeling for a dragon.

Finally, he'd settled near his mother. She had mixed feelings; her heart ached that Battlewing was no longer here. They had said their words before he left, knowing the dangers but still expecting he would return and lead them back to Arcus. She felt diminished at his absence. She also wished he'd been here to see this day. Their strong, wilful son would be taking his place and protecting the royals. Not that Queen Silvarna needed protecting.

The Queen had come to her as soon as they felt the passing of Battlewing. They had flown away from the sadness of the others and found a place to mourn privately. They had settled in the shadow of a mountain and heads touching, they had shared the pain, blue against red. Their minds had become one as she felt Silvarna take some of the pain away. They mourned the loss of Battlewing, a great general, the loss of a husband, a father, a friend, the loss of time. Finally, they had shared their memories, the happy times, the birth of Bluewing and the joy and pride. The times Kyanite had wondered about the future for their son with no females being born since arriving on Suntra. Never to know love. But they had faith in Pathanclaw. He would find a way one day, they hoped, before it was too late.

As the sunrise touched the mountains, and the mist rose from the ground, they parted. Stiff from the many hours of stillness, they stretched their wings, before gracefully rising into the air and returning to the group. Kyanite accepted the condolences from the others as they settled to remember Battlewing and all his great deeds. This day would be spent in remembrance.

Bluewing had moved nearer his mother, and they had touched faces. She would make sure he was ready for the challenges. They would make Battlewing proud, and one day, when she made the long flight to the gem cave, she would be reunited with her love and they would rejoice. It was her choice. She could go now and none would question her or stop her; it was the right of a dragon when they'd lost their mate. But she would see their son and families safe, then maybe, maybe, she would join her husband and let her magic strengthen future dragons so they could thrive.

The next morning, Bluewing looked over the landscape of his temporary home – the snow-tipped mountains were majestic. He had made his choice. He dropped silently down off the mountain and returned to the group as the General, no longer a youngling. His best friend Pathandon had moved through time for them, so Bluewing would protect his family and continue their training. He would become, no, he was, the General, as was expected.

The others were waiting for him. They lined the mountainside, an intimidating sight. Bluewing could feel the excitement of the younglings being part of a historic moment, and ceremony they had only ever heard about in the stories. He was the rightful replacement for his father. It was his right as a Blue, no-one would take that from him. Queen Silvarna was at the front of the group, as Bluewing manoeuvred himself so that he was hovering in the middle of the two dragon lines spanning the canyon. He strengthened his resolve and rode through the wall of coloured fire.

He felt the heat, but it didn't touch his scales. No single flame broke his resolve. Red, Blue, Green, Gold and Silver challenged him. Roaring his victory, Bluewing flew out of the end. He was soon joined by the other dragons as they celebrated this momentous occasion. The new general had been chosen. He had passed the test. He would lead the dragons. When Pathanclaw and Pathandon returned with the lost females to Arcus, they would be ready, and once again dragons would thrive. He held on to this dream while his mother felt immense pride but also sadness, her son was no longer a youngling.

Bluewing returned from his memories and was about to answer Queen Silvarna's question about the younglings' training, but there was a murmuring at the back of the group. Silvarna frowned. It wasn't like anyone to interrupt, especially at an official gathering. She looked into the air and her keen dragon eyes spotted one of the guardians of the gems flying from the direction of the caves. Since they'd arrived here so long ago, they had only seen one of the Black dragons once, when Battlewing had insisted that they practice the battle formation, and they had made a rare appearance. Silvarna knew it had been difficult for Pathanclaw to persuade them to take part, but he needed everyone to be aware how serious it was and that they had to be ready. The sight of the black dragon was not good news.

Ember circled a few times before landing near Queen Silvarna.

"My Queen, I would speak with you alone."

Silvarna considered this. It wasn't in their nature to be secretive. The dragons shared everything. But she knew he wouldn't have requested a private meeting without good reason. She wanted the other dragons to be focused on their plans. She wished Pathanclaw was here. Silvarna nodded but made one demand.

"Please, meet me at my home. General Bluewing, with me. The general should be present."

Ember nodded, and Queen Silvarna and General Bluewing left the others speculating about their fate.

Chapter 3 – Arcus

Raykan woke feeling stiffer than he'd ever remembered in his long life. The freezing cold stone floor felt like sharp icicles were stabbing into his body, trying to pierce his already thin skin, which had been ravaged by fire all those years ago. The scars were stretched so tight that any small movement felt like it would tear them apart.

The noise from the shackles on his hands and feet reverberated around the small cell in the castle dungeon. The fortress on Arcus had been built to hold more than just the royal family. His thoughts went to Prince Villian. He felt sure he'd made it through the portal. Everything in his heart and mind told him the protector of Arcus was alive. He gave a moments thanks to whatever Gods were listening – to protect the young boy and to wish his quest every success; the lives of everyone on Arcus depended on the prince returning with the dragons and restoring order.

Raykan managed to get his body settled against the filthy smelling cell. It was damp and fetid from past inhabitants. He doubted they brought in the maids to clean down here. This made him smile, and he felt better for it. He was weary to the bone. He could see why humans were not meant to live for thousands of years and he welcomed the day his eyes would close for the final time. But his duty and penance were not over yet. Sending Prince Villian through the portal was only the start. He had to be here to see the dragons and peace return once again to the world of Arcus. To restore the balance, which he had unknowingly helped to destroy with his youthful exuberance and desire to live forever. How naive he had been.

Footsteps made him sit up straighter, and pain shot through his damaged body, making him cry out. But his cry was lost in the sounds of the dungeons, which were only now reaching his ears. He'd tried to close his mind to everything. Moans and the smell of terror were so thick he could almost taste it. He needed to escape this place. But the magic he coveted was drained. Opening the portal and placing Prince Villian on an uncertain path had taken its toll. It would be days before his strength returned and he would be able to use his magic to escape. He just hoped he could survive long enough to put his next plan into action.

He looked up as a key was turned in the wooden door. As it opened, it cast in a little light from the candlelit corridor. He chose not to look at the filth it would reveal on the floor. He also preferred to meet his jailors face on. The slight hooded figure closed the door quietly behind them, leaving it ajar, a sliver of light penetrating the darkness. As the figure reached Raykan, they knelt and placed a lamp down as quietly as they could, the strike of a match and the flamed revealed Princess Cartina, Villian's betrothed.

"My lady, what are you doing in such a place? It is dangerous for you to be here. You must leave at once." His voice was croaky due to the ceremony, and he attempted to clear it.

Lady Cartina smiled; her pale marble face reminded him so much of Prince Villian's mother. Her kind brown eyes were damp as she looked him over.

"What have they done to you?"

"Never mind me," Raykan said more sharply than he meant, as he saw her flinch. Her expression hadn't changed at the sight of him, which most were wont to do. The scars on his face were not for the eyes of a maiden. He softened his voice, "Lady Cartina, please, you must leave and quickly."

"Don't worry. I have people loyal to me. Well, they are loyal to my betrothed at least. When I heard that you'd been brought here, I had to come to see what I could do. I know Prince Villian would want me to do everything I could to help his friend. Please, what can I do?"

Raykan eyed her with respect. This slight young girl had a strength that belied her age and appearance.

"How long have I been here?"

"Two days."

Raykan was not surprised. No wonder he'd been stiff; he hadn't moved since they'd shoved him in here. But that meant he would soon be able to use his powers to escape.

"Quickly, tell me what has happened to Ironhand and Valivar?"

The Lady looked confused.

"Sorry, I forget no-one knows or remembers his real name. Valivar is the Keeper of Books."

Lady Cartina nodded.

"I have spoken to Villian's Master Sword and Dyana. They have assured me they are safe."

"You have been busy, Lady Cartina."

He could just see the slight blush on her marble skin. Villian's powers of judgement had clearly been working their magic. They would be a formidable match. If they survived.

"Lady, I must insist that you leave before you are discovered. I will leave here in two days' time, and if it is safe to do so, I will meet you at the edge of the forest near the burnt wasteland. You know where I mean?"

She nodded. "Do you need me to do anything?"

Raykan was loath to bring her into further danger, and he knew Villian would disapprove, but this girl had shown herself to be resourceful and brave. Something they would all need in the coming battles.

"Let Morbark know the plans. He will see you safe and make sure Ironhand and Valivar meet us there. We need to escape the main castle and await the return of Villian. We must prepare his army and be ready."

Lady Cartina left some food and gave him a skein of water to drink from. "Sorry, I cannot leave it. Drink as much as you can."

Raykan waved his hand. He was grateful for what she had done. After he'd drunk as much as his stomach could take, he handed it back. She stood, and without saying a word, she bent down and kissed his forehead lightly before putting out the light and leaving him once again to the darkness.

An hour passed as he focused on healing himself enough to escape. It wouldn't take much. The spells were already appearing in his mind. It was like invisible ink re-emerging on to the page with the right magic, the words slowly revealing themselves and settling back into his memory. The sound of a sword being dragged across the wide stone passageway outside his cell drew his attention, and he frowned at the disturbance as a knot formed in his stomach. If they killed him before he had had the chance to regain his powers, all would be lost. The bolt was drawn, and the door opened slowly. Raykan couldn't help but glance up at the door. It wasn't Lady Cartina coming back; he was certain of that. The girl had already mastered the art of stealth.

"Well, well, well. It's nice to see you awake, Raykan. It's been too long."

Raykan took in the man before him, the greasy hair, filthy clothes, and nasty smile. A man who had the King's ear and did his dirty work.

"Baynard."

The Children – Luminosa

E verything had finally settled down after the children had escaped during the Festival of Time. Kyla had realised why Star had asked all the children to let off fireballs simultaneously. The Masters had looked shocked but not angry, which had terrified Kyla more than the four children disappearing at the time.

A couple of the weaker children went missing before their thirteenth birthdays soon after the Festival of Time. It wasn't unusual but more disappeared than they were expecting. The children often convinced themselves they had forgotten how old they were, and the Masters were taking them because the child had lied about their age. It coincided with more new children turning up in camp than ever had before. These children seemed different though, more defiant; sadly, they didn't last long in the camp. Most didn't even make it to the training rooms. Some of the older ones tried to warn them, but one morning the disobedient ones had gone. In the night, the Masters had come. The Masters didn't seem to care about walking the doomed children through the camp anymore. The children just disappeared. They all felt uneasy, and a quietness settled over them when they weren't training, wondering if they would be next.

The children's' training carried on as they all wondered where the others had disappeared to when they had gone through the portal, and what was going to happen to the ones left behind. Star and Thanan were liked by most, and Triana's stalwart companions seemed happier without her there. The new children mingled with the others and looked relieved. During the day, Kyla gathered a small group together to talk about what had happened. The Masters rarely entered the camp during the day. The children all knew what to do, and it was their job to make sure everyone did as they were told.

"What do you think happened to Triana?" one of the older boys asked.

"Well, I really shouldn't be talking about this," Kyla said.

The gathered group of five leaned in closer. It wasn't often they had new information to share.

"A few weeks before Triana left, she told me she'd been summoned to see the Masters and they'd given her a great task to do, but she would have to pretend everything was normal, and when it happened, she would have to act like she didn't know anything," Kyla whispered.

"That doesn't make sense." One of the girls said before biting her food ball. She sat up as the juice dripped down her chin onto the mossy floor.

"That's disgusting. You look like Star; she used to do that all the time to the new children."

"I'm going to do the same until Star comes back. We all need cheering up."

"Do you think Star will come back?" the boy asked.

"Yes, of course she will," a boy called Lahall said. "I heard one of the other children say they would come back one day and rescue us."

Kyla felt she was losing the group as the other children all spoke at once. It wasn't often she held the attention of the children, as Triana always demanded to be the centre of attention.

"It does make sense," she said loudly, so they stopped their conversations. Once she had their full attention again, she continued, "It's obvious she was sent to spy on the others."

"Do you know where they went?"

"Another world, in another time."

The children gasped. Kyla wasn't quite sure this was true, but it was called the Festival of Time, so it stood to reason it had something to do with time and apparently, the children all came from different places, so it also stood to reason there were different worlds.

"Imagine being able to travel to another time. We could go back to before we were taken and tell our parents, and they would be able to stop us from being stolen," said the young girl.

Kyla and the Galan looked at each other, not wanting them to feel the disappointment, as some of the children remembered their parents letting them go. In her hut, one of the children had cried out every night, pleading with her mother not to send her away. It was heart-breaking; although maybe some of them were better off here, even if they did get taken again when they turned thirteen. Perhaps it was a better life than being unwanted. The Masters wanted them in their own way.

Kyla carried on with her story, "Triana couldn't resist telling me that she had been chosen for this special mission and to expect her to come back."

"But why would you come back if you managed to escape from this place?" the girl asked.

One of the quieter boys said, "Well, we do get to do cool things like having creatures, and some get to learn magic." He blushed as all eyes turned to him.

The girl had finished her food ball and was now wiping her hands on the mossy floor, removing all the juice. "I'm going to get a dragon soon like Star did. Every day I go into training and say, 'Today will be the day,' and I'm going to teach it loads of things like Star did. She had the best creature. I don't want one of those stupid lizards."

"Star, this, Star that. Are you in love with Star?" Kyla couldn't help but let some of her old self come back.

Triana would be proud, but it made her ashamed. "Sorry I said that. I didn't mean it. I'm just jealous. Star's Dragon was really cool."

The girl smiled her forgiveness.

The boy looked into the sky, "It's time to go back. Shall we meet up again later? I want to hear more about what happened."

Kyla nodded. She got up and started walking towards the caves. She'd tried to talk to her worm about what had happened, but he avoided the question. It was rare they could ask a question and get a straight answer. It was the most frustrating thing about learning magic. It was all about forming and shaping the mind, to expand it with information but also connect the pathways so the magic could flow through the mind, from thought to action. She didn't quite understand it, but she had been doing well with her training. She'd mastered a few of the spells now. At the back of her mind, she wondered why they were allowed to learn magic. Surely, they would be a threat to the Masters one day.

Then she thought about the Suckers. It was clever that they couldn't perform magic in the camp unless under supervision. But Thanan, Star, Pol and Triana had managed somehow. Kyla thought their friend Pol had something to do with it. They were strange, and the other children were wary of Pol, despite their tiny frame. Kyla often saw Pol running in the woods; it always made her happy to see it for some reason. She always thought the place seemed lighter when Pol was around.

Kyla arrived at the cave, and after walking her usual path through the tunnels, she lay down in the boat. This was her only refuge. In the boat, no-one could touch her, could make her do anything. She was just her. She would always try and hold her memories here. It was like she stored them in the lights and not in her mind, then nothing could take them away.

She remembered a lot more than she had ever told anyone, even her best friend, Galan. The Masters punished the ones who spoke about their past. Her memories were her lifeline; one day, she would get back home to the rolling fields and the farm she loved. Her mother, father and brothers would be waiting for her. They would welcome her home, and she would show them magic tricks.

Her younger brother would be getting tall now; he was born like a foal – his legs so long, waiting for his body to grow into them. It would be hard on the farm without her to help, although she left at seven or eight and had been on Luminosa four or five years. It was hard to keep track of time. Whenever new children arrived, she hoped one day she would see one of her siblings but felt shame at that hope, knowing what would become of them if they shared the same fate as her. But she needed the feel of home, just one touch, one smell. It would be soon time for her to leave. She didn't think she would go back home then. Why would they be sent home with all this knowledge? She thought maybe they died when the Masters took them. She shivered and not just from the coldness in the cave. She and Galan had spoken about leaving; maybe they should have left with Star. Perhaps they wouldn't ever get another chance.

Chapter 4 – Luminosa

Villian and Thanan shared a look. They were both getting a bit sick of disappearing and arriving in a place they didn't know. Something felt very wrong. The boys looked around at the same time. They expected to hear Star shouting and raging right about now, but there was only silence and an empty space where Star and Dragon should have been.

"What happened to Star?" Villian said.

"I saw that evil dragon dung, Triana, messing with her talisman before we all disappeared. She must have put a protection spell over them or something. We must go back," Thanan shouted.

Thanan's heart ached for Star.

"How did we disappear, and where are we?" Villian said. This wasn't what he expected to happen at all.

"Pol and I moved us here." Pathanclaw's words formed in their minds.

Thanan turned, he'd forgotten Pol was even there, and he realised their fingers were no longer digging into his back and they were standing at the side of the cave.

"I can answer where we are," Thanan said, recognising it now. He looked around properly. "These must be the caves Tobias told me about. He told us to hide in here if things went wrong during The Festival of Time."

"That must mean there is a way out?" Villian was already forming a plan in his mind. "We are still on Luminosa then?"

"Yes, hold on whilst I get down. Pathandon, would you

mind?" Thanan asked. The cave roof was closer to his head than he would like and water was dripping down his back. There was a glow coming from a large tunnel to the right. He suspected he knew where it would lead to. He could also hear water in the distance. As he slid down the dragon, he noticed the tattoo on his arm had disappeared.

"Look." Thanan held up his arm to the others. "Villian, is yours still there?"

Pathandon and Pathanclaw lowered their wings and Thanan and Villian slid down and landed on the cave floor.

Villian pulled up his sleeve to reveal the vibrant tattoo still on his arm. "It must be because we've returned here. I suppose you don't need the power to get back here now you're already here. Like a key you no longer need because the door is unlocked."

Thanan nodded, thinking it made perfect sense. He felt a bit naked without it, though. He'd felt safer knowing he had something which made him special.

They moved towards the light, eager to be outside. The cave felt like a tomb, despite its size. Pol moved ahead, and Villian spoke, "Wait for us, Pol. It might not be safe."

But Pol smiled and beckoned them to follow. Thanan didn't hesitate, this wasn't how he thought this day was going to work out. He thought they would arrive, the dragons would do their thing, they would free the children and female dragons, perhaps even kill the Masters if they had to. This was going to much harder than he thought. He cursed his naivety – he didn't deserve to be amongst such brave companions. He could already see Villian was forming a plan. He was trained, a Prince; what did Thanan know about anything.

"*We will do it together, Thanan.*" Pol's words entered his mind, and he looked up to see them smiling at him. So, Pol could no longer talk again now they were back on Luminosa. Thanan felt like he needed time to process all these things that were happening, but everything moved so fast. They should have made Triana tell them about the talisman; why hadn't Pathanclaw insisted? Maybe the talisman was an alarm to alert the Masters of their arrival. He was surprised King Pathanclaw had made such a mistake, and now Star and Dragon were paying for it. His mind spiralled. What about the book Villian had? Perhaps that would help them. Too many questions and no time to answer them as usual.

"Pol is right, Thanan." Pathandon's clear strong voice swirled in his mind. *"Sorry to invade your space, but you're making my head hurt."*

"Sorry, Pathandon," Thanan said. Over the months of training with Pathandon, he'd found it easier to communicate via minds, as came naturally to him and Star with Pol. His heart sank again at the thought of Star. He would not allow her to return only to die. He wouldn't.

"You're worried about your friend. As are we. It's only natural. But emotion needs to be set aside so we can focus, rescue her and set things right on Luminosa. I admit that I was not prepared for the Masters to behave in such a callous way, to use the children as a shield."

"This is my error." King Pathanclaw entered the conversation. *"I should have known they would have no regard for the children's welfare. It was I who was not as prepared as I should have been. It seems time has made me forget the real evil we face. Perhaps the joy of having the female dragons returned to us have overshadowed my decisions. What has happened to our friends is my burden to bear, Thanan."*

As they communicated, the group followed Pol, the dragons moving clumsily through the large tunnels. Eventually, they arrived at the entrance of the cave and looked out into the oasis Pol had brought them to on that last night which felt like years ago. The colours so vivid, Villian had to shield his eyes from the brightness before him. Birds flew everywhere, the roar of the waterfall falling into the deep green lake at the bottom accompanied the white frothing waves of water.

"Wow," said Villian. "What is this place? Are we safe here?"

"Yes," Thanan answered, "Pol brought us here once. I'm not quite sure what it is, but we were safe from the Masters. Safe from everything."

Villian looked at Pol, who had wandered into the forest and was dancing delightedly with birds flying around them. He wondered at Pol's abilities. If they had so much power, why didn't they use it to release the children? It didn't make sense.

"Can the Masters get to us in here?" Villian asked again.

"I don't think they can find us here." Thanan shrugged. What did he know, but it felt safe here, in this mysterious place. He felt despair wash over him. What were they going to do? How were they to save the other children and dragons on Luminosa? Thanan didn't like to say he thought it was impossible. The Masters didn't care about the children; he knew this better than anyone. The children knew this, so why didn't they help them? The dragons should have tried harder, could have burnt the Masters to a crisp, used more magic, and it would have all been over. He knew why; fear. He could see it in their eyes as he looked over them in the split second before they had disappeared. He'd seen Galan open-mouthed as he saw dragons for the first time.

"Right," Villian said, "King Pathanclaw, it's clear that you know one of the Masters. We need to know the enemy so we can fight them. If we know them, we can find their weaknesses. I think you have long been holding back, and we have a right to know the dangers we face."

Thanan wondered if Prince Villian had gone too far with this surprising outburst, taken his developing relationship with the King of all dragons beyond his reasonable demands. Pathanclaw could burn him to a crisp, and Villian couldn't stop him. Thanan thought he might be able to get a protection spell up in time, but then what? His skills were limited as he was finding out. Maybe if Pathanclaw suspected, he should have told them more before they left the planet that could be Arcus of the past or future. According to Pathanclaw, the portal would only stay open for a year. They had already wasted months, and he, Star and Pol were back where they started and, in even more danger, and Star and Dragon were now missing. His temper flared. Before he could say anything, he felt a gentle hand on his arm.

"It's okay." Pol's gentle voice came into his mind.

Thanan forced himself to relax. "Will it be okay though, Pol? What did I do to help my friends? Nothing. Why did I let Triana join Star on the back of Dragon? I should have put aside my hatred of her and kept her close. Not let one of my best friends carry her, and now she's probably hurting Star and Dragon. Who knows what they are going to do to her? It's just not fair!"

Thanan realised he sounded like a child, as tears threatened to spill. But he was a child. He'd only turned thirteen a few months ago and had spent most of his life on this planet being taught by a giant worm and controlled by Masters. It was no wonder he didn't know what to do. He kicked a small rock in frustration, and it rebounded noisily against the wall of the cave.

"Well, I suppose we won't have to go to them. With the noise you're making, it will bring them right to us," Villian exclaimed.

Thanan whirled in anger, but Villian's face was sympathetic, not judgemental, and the anger turned to blushes.

"Sorry. I'm worried about Star, that's all."

Villian moved closer and clasped his hand on Thanan's

shoulder. "I know. We all are. We will do everything we can to rescue Star and Dragon. I promise."

Pathandon had been watching these young humans and was surprised to find himself feel the same anger as Thanan did. He wanted to fly to these Masters and burn them until not even ash remained. It was an odd feeling. He was used to hearing and feeling the thoughts of other dragons, but with humans, everything seemed heightened emotionally and strangely their mental connection more natural than he had ever thought possible.

He'd grown up with the story of humans, and the future of dragons had always been to leave all he had ever known on Suntra and return to Arcus. The younglings grew up knowing their planet was only a temporary home. It felt odd to be born somewhere you knew wasn't yours to call home. He felt for this young human. Thanan had been stolen from his family and lived without direction on this strange planet.

Pathanclaw looked at his grandson as he watched the young human with whom he would now be bound for the rest of his life. His grandson didn't know this yet, but the same happened to him and Raykan. They were bound. A link had been created which neither of them really understood. He'd noticed his grandson move closer to Thanan when Villian had challenged him. Pathanclaw was pleased and saddened. Human life was so short, it was difficult for a dragon to comprehend when a friend left them so soon. He shook himself; the time for melancholy was not now. They needed to plan, and fast.

"Thanan, do you or Pol recognise where we are in relation to the Masters. Where do you think they will be holding Star and where are the dragons?"

"Finally, some action," Villian said, with a lightness to his voice which no-one believed. He was as worried as the others about Star and how they were going to tackle the Masters now they had lost the element of surprise.

Thanan wiped his face and made his way to the centre of the group, followed by Pol. He drew the dagger Villian had trained him with, and he drew a map in the sand before them as best he could. They had walked a long way to get to this place with Pol, and he couldn't say he'd been paying attention to exactly where they were but he knew the general direction. Villian peered over his shoulder, and recognition flared in his memory. It was one of the maps Raykan had shown him. How had he known the landscape of Suntra? Now, however, was not the time to share that.

"Where do you think they will be holding, Star?" Villian asked.

Thanan pointed to an area on the other side of the sleeping quarters in camp. "We used to sleep here, and whenever one of the children did anything wrong, this was where they were taken. It's just inside the forest, and the cells are underground."

"Have you ever been in them?" Villian asked.

"No. Star has a few times though." Thanan couldn't help but grin and, Villian matched him; knowing Star's personality, it was not surprising. She wasn't one to follow the rules. But this came with a wave of sadness for Thanan as he knew her time imprisoned there had scared her.

"Well, we have to hope they are keeping her alive as they will want to find out what she knows, and she and Dragon will be useful. I really wish Star had a name for Dragon. It seems silly to keep calling her that," Villian said. The last, almost to himself.

Thanan nodded. Try making Star do anything she didn't want to, he thought, and he could hear a slight chuckle from Pathandon – if dragons could chuckle. Thanan really needed to work on closing his mind. Pathandon looked at him apologetically; he had promised to avoid listening in on Thanan's thoughts. Thanan smiled to let him know he wasn't upset, and strangely, he wasn't.

"So Thanan, judging by your map, the female dragons are at the edge of the forest in this direction, and they are protected by men, but you don't think they are Masters. Before you say it, I know we discussed this before we left, but we are going to have to change our plans, so it does no harm to confirm these points."

"Yes, Pol and Star were the ones who saw them."

Pol's head bowed, and it was Thanan's turn to put a comforting arm around his friend. He'd seen the pain and anger Pol felt when they had discovered the suckers who stopped their magic were actually dragons, chained and enslaved, as were the children. Not for the first time, Thanan wondered at Pols powers. Why couldn't they just kill them all? But he'd seen how they were with nature; Pol wouldn't kill anything living, no matter what it was, maybe, all they could do was protect.

"Do we need to split up?" Villian asked Pathanclaw.

"It was not what I wanted, but I think that would be wise. We have to be smart, and the Masters reach can only stretch so far. If we release the female dragons, this gives us an advantage. Although they may be weak, I would still rather have them on our side. The Masters will know this."

"Thanan, how long do you think it would take you to get out of the caves?" Pathanclaw enquired.

"It depends on how many twists and turns there are in the caves. Maybe a couple of hours."

"And from there, you can get to the camp and the children?"

"Yes, but as I've told you, there's a boat and only one person can travel in it at a time. Someone must pull you through the other side. It's difficult to pull yourself through. So, I wouldn't be able to get help that way, and they would know we were coming."

Pathanclaw thought for a few moments and turned to look at Pol.

"Do you think you will be able to block the Masters magic?"

Pol nodded but looked unsure.

Thanan thought he could guess what she was thinking, "If Pol does that, it could mean you won't be able to do magic?"

"We don't need magic to burn them to a crisp or bite their heads off," Pathandon said.

The two boys grinned, but Pol grimaced.

"Here is what I think we should do. Pathandon and I are too easy to see. The Masters will be ready for us, and despite being able to fly silently when we choose, it will not help us if we are attacked in the air with you on our backs. You have learned a lot in a short time but entering a full magic battle is not one any of you are ready for."

Pathandon and Villian bristled at this suggested rebuke of their abilities.

Pathanclaw tried to placate them. "I do not mean it to be a judgement. You've all worked hard, but in battle, as Villian knows, if you don't identify and recognise your weaknesses, then your enemy will. I believe the Masters will expect us to fight back and together."

Pathanclaw paused, considering. The others waited. Finally, he said, "You're right, Villian. We need to split up."

Chapter 5 – Suntra

Queen Silvarna watched as General Bluewing sent the other dragons away to continue their training. They left to meet the guardian in her chamber. It was a testament to these changing times and the dangers that lay ahead that they were not meeting with the whole council.

It did not take long for them to settle, as they were all anxious about this meeting. Silvarna requested that the Black dragon, Ember, updated them, if Silvarna's memory was serving her correctly. The Black dragons rarely used names. Guardians didn't often need to be addressed and were superstitious about others knowing their names. The guardian updated them on the new danger they faced.

"The gems are disappearing?" Bluewing asked in disbelief.

Not only were the Black dragons elusive, it seemed this extended to their words. The gravity of his words made the silence stretch on. Bluewing looked at his queen, trying to understand if it was his place to speak again. But what would he say? The gems were disappearing, they were the essence of a dragon's magic. How could this be happening? Who was taking them, why and how? He could hear similar questions in his queen's mind and decided his father would have demanded to know.

Bluewing puffed out his chest, thinking of his duty and asked the questions they needed answers to.

"I do not know why. But there is no doubt someone is

stealing the power from the gems and using it for magic," the guardian answered.

"What does this mean for King Pathanclaw and Pathandon?"

"At the moment they are safe. This has never happened before, so we cannot be sure how quickly that will change."

Silence moved uncomfortably amongst them. How could someone else use the magic from the gems? It was not possible. It was unthinkable that their magic could be stolen without their knowledge. What would this mean for King Pathanclaw's plan to return to Arcus? They needed the gems. They were the essence of a dragon and the power needed to move through time.

"I believe King Pathanclaw and Pathandon have moved in time. Wouldn't that account for the gems being used at a quicker pace?" The others turned to see Longsong, a Green Elder waiting in the shadows. Even the guardian was surprised. The Greens lived in the gem caves and were even more secretive than the Blacks, their minds lost to magic.

"Yes, but that was a possibility I had discussed with King Pathanclaw. But this doesn't account for the amount. Someone else is using them."

"How can this be?" Bluewing asked. He didn't know enough. Despite dragons passing on their knowledge, this didn't include everything which happened in a dragon's life. He could not remember any stories where the gems had been stolen or simply disappeared.

"They must have access to the gem cave on Arcus."

The shock of the implication was felt by all. If Longsong was right, then the cave on Arcus was compromised. Before they left, they had sealed the gem cave with powerful magic. It should never have been able to be found by humans. His treachery could only be performed by humans. No dragon would risk the cave being discovered.

"What can we do?" Silvarna asked. "What do you need from us?"

"I do not know yet, my Queen. I felt the council needed to know. I will return now and I request your presence and General Bluewing at first light tomorrow."

"We will be there. Thank you for your council, Guardian of the Gems and to you, Longsong. These words are difficult to hear but we need to know the dangers we face."

"There is much you need to know. Secrets will not aid our plight now," Longsong added mysteriously before leaving.

"We will not discuss this with the others. I know this goes against our nature but we need to have all the facts before we decide our next move," Queen Silvarna informed Bluewing.

He agreed but worried about what this meant to their kin and their safety on Suntra. Longsong had more to reveal. What secrets could there possibly be, and how would this affect their plans? Would they have to leave before King Pathanclaw and Pathandon returned? The Elders could open the portal again, but each time it used precious gems and without the cure, and the females returning to Arcus, would be a death sentence. They needed to remain strong and stay on Suntra for when they returned.

Bluewing left, there was nothing else they could do. They agreed to call a council meeting tomorrow after they had visited the gem cave to discover the secrets Longsong held.

Chapter 6 – Arcus

"Hello, Raykan. Nice to see you again. It's been a while." Baynard said.

Raykan said nothing to the odious worm. The memory of him being the hand of the king that pushed him into the fire all those years ago made his skin tingle unpleasantly.

"Nothing to say for yourself? Well, I'm sure we can change that."

Raykan looked him up and down in contempt. He wasn't afraid of what they would do to him. He'd felt enough pain and sorrow to know he could withstand it. He simply didn't have time for this small-minded man and his torturous pleasures. He was lucky that the Lady Cartina's visit had preceded this one. He was armed with information, Baynard didn't know he had.

Baynard moved further into the cell and hooked a lantern onto an iron ring on the wall near the door. Baynard looked at the flame, stared at Raykan's fire scarred face and smiled.

"Don't worry. Not today my friend. I wanted to have a little chat with you before we get down to the real business. It would go well for you if you told me exactly what I need to know."

Raykan knew that it didn't matter what he told the king's aide, this man would torture him regardless. It was his nature. But he might learn something. So what was the harm in a little conversation? He had nowhere to be right now. All he need do was heal, and be ready.

"The King is very keen to learn where his only son is, after we managed to kill one of your treasonous accomplices and imprison another a few nights ago." He smiled. "You might have heard his screams." He paused, for dramatic effect, to let the anxiety take hold. Mentally Raykan thanked Lady Cartina once again. Without the prior knowledge, this would have been worrying news. "We know Prince Villian was with you, but it was only your body we found in the cave. Where is Prince Villian?"

Raykan weighed up his options. Baynard was clearly lying, as long as Lady Cartina was telling the truth and this wasn't a trick. He had no choice but to trust Villain's betrothed. Despite his young age, the prince was a shrewd judge of character. He had trusted her enough to tell her about his quest. There was no harm in them knowing.

"I aided Prince Villian to go on a quest to save Arcus. Your king and his subjects are clearly not capable of saving our people. The prince has more backbone than any of you will ever possess and courage..."

A swift kick in the side silenced him, and a fit of coughing ensued.

"You think you're so clever, Raykan. Out there in the woods, believing your meetings with the prince were a secret, that the King had no knowledge of what was going on. Your scheming and grand plans which you burrowed into his mind. Using his mother as leverage to make Villian your puppet. Fools!"

Baynard's laugh made Raykan feel uneasy. They had been careful over the years, but clearly it had not been enough.

"We have been watching and waiting to see what you would do. To catch you in the act so to speak. It was unfortunate we met some resistance on the night. Unexpected but it was dealt with swiftly."

Unconsciously, Baynard's hand moved to his stomach. He had been injured then. It was a shame the blow had not been fatal. For all he that loathed this man, Raykan knew he was a skilful fighter. But Ironhand and The Keeper of Books were a match. He wouldn't have expected the librarian to be a force. Raykan knew that the Keeper had many skills as well as being gifted or cursed with the longevity of life as he was.

"The King is not pleased that we do not have his precious only son, the heir to Kingdom. The marriage vows have not yet been confirmed and I'm sure I don't need to tell you that we need the might of the other families to unite against the one enemy."

"That is good. Prince Villian and I have the same purpose. To defeat the enemy in our midst and restore peace to the land once again."

Baynard sneered, "Fairy tales and stupid dreams. You've been filling his head and your own with nonsense for far too long, Raykan. I told the King many years ago we should have burnt down your filthy hut with you in it. But he insisted that his son follow this dead-end path. I'm at a loss as to why."

"Ah, but in the end, it's turned out the path had another way out. A direction you and your small-minded peasants could never foresee. You should be ashamed to have let this great house be reduced to desperate scraps and forcing two young people to marry to save your necks. Thank the dragons, Prince Villian is like his grandfathers of old. Like his mother. They knew how to rule a kingdom."

"Dragons! You fool," Baynard spat, spittle falling down his chin, "what do you know about the families of old? Read that in a book did you? Well, never again, I've seen to that." He sneered again.

"What do you mean?" Dread filled Raykan's heart.

"We need something to feed the fires in the castle. With the Keeper dead, I finally persuaded the king that we had no use for a library which has been turning the minds of the Prince. Tonight, we will hold a gathering and burn every damn book in that place. But first..."

Baynard barked an order and a guard moved from the corridor and handed the aide a book. Raykan's heart sank. He knew what the guard held. The dragon clasp caught the light from the lantern. Raykan tried to think of a spell, but he was too weak. He needed more time for the words to join in his mind. Too many were missing.

"Too long you have been allowed to poison minds with your talk of magic, Raykan. Thankfully, the disappearance of his son has made the king keen to finally seek out the heretics and make them pay. Books are the devil's work and they shall no longer be allowed to turn the minds of men."

With this, Baynard opened the clasps and set the book on the floor. Raykan could see the coloured images and letters, still as fresh as the day they had been written. Baynard reached up into his pocket and pulled out a length of lighting wick and touched it to the lantern flame. The wick caught quickly and keeping eye contact, Baynard slowly moved the flame towards the book.

"Tell me everything you know or I will burn this book and you with it."

The Children – Luminosa

The Masters called them to the clearing just beyond the camp. There was excitement but also fear. Galan was desperately worried about Kyla – would he ever see her again? In his heart he knew the answer, but it didn't stop the hope. She was a strong person, surely she would come up with something. But no-one had ever returned. He felt sick about Kalen as well. They had all tried to cover up for him but he wasn't developing his ability as well as the others. He should have had a creature by now. He had spent longer than the others in the training rooms because it didn't come naturally to him.

The air crackled and the light grew brighter. Galan squinted. He could see something. A pinprick of light in mid-air, as if someone had shone a torch through time. But how could this be. There wasn't a festival, no ceremony had been performed. Was Triana coming back as they had thought? Some of the children tried to move, but found they were fixed in place. The chanting beside them made them realise the Masters had put a spell on them. Galan was sure that whatever was coming through that portal, the children were going to be used as a shield. The Masters had not gathered them in the shadows of the trees for nothing.

The children would have run if they could, but they were waiting for the signal to move. In a flash of light, three huge dragons were before them. Galan's eyes widened at the sight before him. They were magnificent. The biggest of them all in the middle, red, carrying a boy;

a smaller red to the left, with another boy. His eyes widened even further as he recognised Thanan. They had come back. He quickly looked to the left and the smallest dragon. It was Star. A great cheer went up as they children spotted them but it turned to a gasp as they watched the unfolding events with horror.

The flames hit the Masters but to their disappointment nothing happened. The Masters motioned the children to form a circle around the seven Masters. The one who had taken Kalen and Kyla still missing. Six of them stood behind the one that was taller than the rest, the one who had led the Festival of Time. The children were hushed and an unnatural silence descended.

The main dragon spoke one name, "Barakar." The children didn't know how they could hear it. Who were the dragons talking about? Was it one of the Masters? The children didn't think of the Master's as having names. The main Master stepped even closer to the dragons, unafraid. Now the children were in place, he'd removed his hood. Only a few of the children could see his face in the shadows. Most were transfixed by the sight before them. The man before him looked young, unremarkable. Disappointment was Galan's thought before he focused back on the dragon.

Magic tingled in the air. It was alive with words, it felt like they were swirling around like the autumn leaves back on Galan's home world. All the Masters were chanting, as the shimmering with the colours of Luminosa, Gold, Silver, Blue, Green, Red, Purple and Black covered the Masters within the circle. The children left outside weren't defenceless, the ones who could do magic had their powers and the ones with dragons and lizards suddenly appeared before them. This meant the Suckers weren't working. The children looked at each and looked at the dragons. What could they do against them? Their friends, the dragons were with them. They had tried to attack the Masters. This meant the dragons were good, had maybe come to save them.

Whilst the children continued to wait, they could feel that the Masters were preparing to attack. The air felt charged with intent. The dragons could see it too. Galan spotted Triana behind Star, she had come back then as well. As he watched, Triana held something in her hands, and he could see she was forming magic. It all seemed to happen at once, a great tide of heat went high up into the air and then dived in the direction of the dragons.

He heard Thanan shout a warning to Star but it was too late, in a blink of an eye the two red dragons disappeared. Star remained with Dragon and Triana. Dragon turned to face the Masters as Star tried to turn and attack Triana. But it was a losing battle. The shield dropped behind them and tentacles of light circled from one of the Masters. It struck Star like a snake striking its victim and she fell across Dragon. Dragon roared but could do nothing to help her. Triana had a knife to Stars throat. In moments, the Masters had a hideous looking contraption secured over Dragon's mouth. It was over as quickly as it began.

The Master whom the dragon had called Barakar, moved in front of Star's Dragon. By the look of anger on his face, Galan would have taken a step back if he could. The Master spoke softly but the words were clear.

"Welcome home, Star. We are so pleased you have returned. It's good to see you have made progress with your Dragon whilst you have been away. We will discuss it later whilst I search for and kill your friends."

The violence in his voice made Galan shudder. He looked at Star but she still had defiance in her eyes, despite the thin trail of blood which was tracking a slow path down her neck. Star spoke, even as the dagger went deeper, "If you let me go, I will show you exactly what my Dragon can do."

A soft laugh met her words, and Triana twisted the dagger in further. The flow became thicker and soaked into Star's tunic. The girl didn't even flinch.

"You will come with me and control your dragon. If it so much as makes a move, I will kill you both without a thought. Do you understand?"

It was Dragon who nodded her head slightly. Speaking for them both and being the more sensible of the two, Galan thought.

Barakar nodded and two of the Masters waited for Triana and Star to dismount. They led them to the place none of the children liked to go. The children were confused by what they had just seen. Their whisperings were silenced by a look. Galan felt frustrated and helpless as he watched them leave. He couldn't help Kyla, Kalen, and now Star. As the group passed by Galan, Star turned, looked directly at him, and mouthed.

Be ready...

Chapter 7 – Luminosa

Star strode back and forth in the small space, fury driving her forward. She looked into the next cell where Dragon was tied to the sides of the wall with giant chains. A huge metal muzzle covered her face, like the ones Star and Pol had seen on the female dragons outside of camp.

She wasn't only furious, Star was angry and scared. How had this happened? They had been prepared to arrive on Luminosa with Pathanclaw and Pathandon. They would destroy the Masters and everything would be alright. The knot of fear she'd had in her stomach since they'd decided to return to Luminosa, flared. Here she was back again in this terrible place, not knowing how her friends were, not knowing her fate.

Star hoped they were okay. She had tried opening her mind but there was nothing. She reasoned there was no way the Masters would let her use her powers. Her friends hadn't had time to do anything before Triana, the evil dragon vomit, had done something. She'd seen it in Thanan's eyes as he'd shouted his warning. Dragon had turned her head but what could they do? The plan had been stupid. The Masters were ready for them. The dragons could not bring themselves to hurt the children to destroy the Masters. They should have been more prepared, should have seen this coming, especially Prince Villian and Pathanclaw. They knew about such things.

Star looked at Dragon and smiled, it made her feel a little better. They would get out of here one way or another, they just had to be smart about it. She was confident the others would have escaped. In fact, she'd seen Pol close their eyes and shimmer, which meant they must have escaped safely. If only she hadn't had that backstabbing Triana behind her. That girl would pay one day, she would make sure of that. Her hand went to her neck where the wound stung, but thankfully the bleeding had stopped. Her top was caked with dried blood.

Her angry footsteps were kicking up dust and Dragon sneezed. It made her laugh and she smiled at her companion. Dragon was bigger now they had both been trained. It wasn't the same as the last time she was here. This time she would escape and then she would make them all pay. Star grabbed hold of her anger, clenching her fist and started to plan. She bent down and peered through the iron bars at Dragon. She'd often wondered why a name had never seemed right. She'd spent what felt like forever thinking about a name, but one had never fitted. The names didn't suit Dragon's personality. But what was a thing without a name? What did it mean that she couldn't think of one? Would Dragon be taken away from her because she didn't deserve her? All mothers named their children. It was strange, despite her young age, she felt Dragon was her child. She had somehow created her with her magic. Using powers, which even now, she didn't really understand.

In the training rooms it had been extremely strict. They were never allowed to practice magic on their own and the moment their creatures came into being, the magic disappeared and their next level of training started; becoming one with their creature and learning to communicate with them. She'd often wondered why they trained their creature, only for them to disappear when they turned thirteen. It made her ache when she thought about being separated from Dragon or her friends. How could the Masters do this to children? Why did they do it?

Why let them create such amazing gifts just to kill them? It didn't make sense.

As she smelt the damp air around her, she recalled the day she'd lain on the grass, during the times Thanan would be concentrating and thinking up questions to ask Tobias. She was glad she'd not been chosen to do magic training. It sounded boring. She'd tried to work on Dragon and get her to tell her what she was thinking. Maybe if she understood Dragon more, then maybe a name would come. It would tell her Dragon's personality. But it just never came.

Dragon looked at her as if she could read her mind. Maybe she could. The link between them was becoming stronger. She'd felt the power of it when they had returned to Luminosa and the magic seemed to return to them all. She hated to see Dragon weighed down with the great iron muzzle and chains. It was so wrong. How could the Master's treat them like this? Why had Triana betrayed them as she had? Why? They had tried to be friends with her, even she had made an effort at Thanan's encouragement, but Triana was just not a likeable person.

When she'd met King Pathanclaw and Pathandon she thought a name would come. She could name Dragon after one of the great dragons of old. That would be a worthy name. She had spoken to Pathanclaw about it one evening after they were all bone weary from the relentless training Villian tasked them with. She was glad she wasn't one of those warriors he'd spoken about, she would have shown him a thing or to. She had to admit though, the training did her good. She had grown up as had Dragon. She had often showed off her growing muscles to an eye roll by Thanan. He would never agree to an arm wrestle anymore. Thoughts of a name came back. Why couldn't she think of one? She was overthinking. Repeating questions. She had to calm down.

Star looked at Dragons back. When Dragon was big enough to take her size and weight it had been the best day of her life. Riding together through the sky. Dragon made a noise and Star focused back in from her thoughts. Star smiled.

"You can hear my thoughts, can't you?"

Dragon tilted her head, her sign that she was listening and agreeing. Star moved closer to the cage and pushed her arm through the small gap and stretched. Her fingertip touching the now solid scales, the soft feathers long since shed. As she stroked Dragon, her thoughts moved back to those days, when they were all practising and soaring high in the sky on the dragons. It was exhilarating to feel so free amongst the clouds. She and Thanan had felt invincible. They had been foolish. Children playing at war.

She closed her eyes feeling comforted by the connection with Dragon. Her mind wandered to the months they'd had in the past. She now realised they were the happiest times of her life so far, but she couldn't seem to focus on them properly now. Her mind kept drifting, as if something was trying to steal her memories, to listen to her thoughts. She shook her head, trying to fight it.

In her mind's eye she saw Prince Villian astride King Pathanclaw. They looked like they fitted together, just like her and Dragon. Thanan and Pathandon looked a little bit awkward, as if neither of them wanted to acknowledge how much they actually enjoyed it. Star couldn't believe that with all the training they'd had, they'd arrived on Luminosa and immediately she had been taken captive and the others had left her. A part of her felt angry at them leaving, but she did understand and she knew they would come for if they could. She hoped they were safe.

When Star had been talking to Pathanclaw she had asked him about the history of the dragons and how they were linked to the gems they had spoken about and how it gave them their magical powers. He had been reluctant to explain more at first but they needed to understand. Any knowledge which could help defeat the Masters was important for them to know.

Star's hand dropped and she stared sightless at the wall, her mind and mouth open. Dragon whined.

Pathanclaw had explained more about the families and the role each of them played. He and Pathandon had been sad when they talked about General Battlewing who had died when they'd arrived. But Pathandon's chest puffed out when he talked of his friend on Suntra called Bluewing, General Battlewing's son. Apparently, he would become the new general as a Blue dragon was always by the side of a royal dragon. She had believed it was her and Dragon's destiny now. They were Blues. Warriors. Defenders. Thanan had muttered something about never hearing the end of it now.

Star talked to Pathanclaw or Pathandon whenever she got chance, making them tell her about the other dragons. The silver dragons were natural hunters with amazing eyesight and if they tipped their bodies at the right angle they could dazzle their prey. She and Dragon had practiced these moves whilst Pathanclaw watched, amused and energised by Star's enthusiasm.

She was fascinated to hear about the dragons who had disappeared from Arcus when they all left. Where had they gone and what were they doing? Were they all dead? Why had they left the other dragons in their hour of need and did Pathanclaw think they would come back? How had the females ended up on Suntra? Did he think it would be safe on Arcus now for the dragons?

Thanan and Villian's soft chuckles had turned to full belly laughs.

"What?" she said, stamping her foot, but her mouth twitched.

Through the laughter Villian had said, "Maybe try and

ask one question at a time Star and that way you might get an answer to each question."

"Pathanclaw is a King, a dragon. Of course he can answer all those questions at once." She'd turned to look at Pathanclaw, who was very slowly edging away from the group. This set the boys off again and as she started walking towards Pathanclaw, he took flight and purposely directed his wings at her so she fell on her backside, much to the hilarity of the boys. Even Pol was laughing, which Star was delighted to see, and she joined in with her friends. The only one who didn't join in was Triana. Often they didn't see her all day as she didn't join in with any of the training. But Star had seen her spying on them on more than one occasion.

But now Dragon whined as he tried to rouse Star.

"Splitting up could be dangerous. Look what happened when we were all together." Thanan said to Pathanclaw.

"Barakar will not expect us to split up. Despite what he has done, the man is a coward."

"Wait, Pathanclaw. You need to explain to us. You know one of the Masters?" Thanan said, realising Villian's question from earlier had been overlooked. One of the Masters had a name? He'd never really thought of them as people. Silly really. They were always a collective term, Masters not individuals, but he supposed it was childish thinking. A way of making them bigger than they were. Not something which could be challenged. A group, not singular.

"We never seem to have the time for explanations. We need to strike as soon as we have a plan. I don't want young Star left with them any longer than needed."

"I think it's them you should be worried about," said Villian, and this made the others smile, despite their worry. Star was a force and Dragon was so much stronger now. Surely the Masters wouldn't risk hurting Star if they could use her against her friends.

Pathanclaw continued, glad that the mood had lightened a little, *"I think you have more chance of saving the children if we are not there. You know the camp and can enter quietly. If you can get the children away, then the Masters have lost their advantage. I propose that Pathandon and I go to save the females and draw any interest from the Masters to us. You can get through the caves and bring the children back here and rescue Star. Do you think you can do it?"*

They all looked at Thanan and he answered King Pathanclaw, "Yes, but we need someone on the other side of the cave to pull the boat through, and like I said, it will take an age for us all to get through."

"I understand, but we need to get the children in a safe place. The Masters will allow training with this going on, so it's unlikely that anyone will be guarding the boats. In the cave, we can protect them more easily. We can bring them here. There is a magic about this place which the outside cannot touch without permission."

Thanan looked unsure. What Pathanclaw said made sense. It would be easier to keep the children safe in the training room. But getting all the children through would be difficult. Pathandon broke his thoughts.

"What if we drop Villian as close as we can to the entrance. If we use a protection spell we can mask our entrance, unlike earlier."

Thanan interrupted, "But the children are unlikely to listen to Villian, they do not know him. It would have to me who spoke with them."

"So, I will secure the main entrance and wait for your signal to pull you through the cave and then we both go and get the children."

"That could work but it's going to take a lot of time. I

already feel we are wasting time talking about it, and what about Star?"

"Once the children are making their way through, we can go and get Star. You said it's not far away. Maybe, when we get closer, you will be able to communicate with her?"

"Maybe. I've tried a few times but I cannot hear her. Can you, Pol?"

Pol shook their head.

Villian turned to Pol. "Pol, are you able to do anything to help? I don't understand what power you have but you seem to be able to get us out of trouble when we need it. Is there nothing you can do to stop the Masters?"

Pol shrugged.

Thanan said, "I think, Pol is unable to intervene unless there is danger. From what I've seen over the years, they are at one with nature and it must include every living thing. I'm not sure Pol would be able to fight them or harm them no matter what they did. Although I won't say no to being rescued. But do you think you could pull the children through, Pol?"

Pol smiled at him, grateful for his understanding and nodded.

"Maybe you're right, Thanan. I don't quite understand it, but then again, I didn't know my dreams of hope of magic or dragons really existed until a few months ago, so what do I know? Are you sure you're strong enough?" Prince Villian said looking down at the diminutive form before him. He'd realised Pol's eyes hadn't changed colour again since the day he'd met them. They were always serious now, he hadn't seen much of this funny, light-hearted Pol the others spoke about."

"Great idea. Pol can do that and we can go and rescue the children. Send them to the cave and go rescue Star." Thanan sounded excited and eager to get moving.

"Right, I think we need to move soon. We cannot delay

much longer and let the Masters get the upper hand once again. Thanan, Villian and Pol we will drop you as close as we can before heading to free the female dragons. We will cause as much disruption as we can so that you can get everyone to safety. Remember, we can still communicate, so if you need us, we will come to you, but this way I hope that we save everyone." Pathanclaw stated.

"Before we leave, I think you need to tell us more about this Barakar. Who is he? Knowing your enemy always makes you stronger in battle," Villian directed his question to Pathanclaw, knowing they were all keen to get moving but this knowledge could make the difference. He was frustrated King Pathanclaw held back information he felt they needed to know.

Pathanclaw knew they deserved an answer. His friends would find out everything in time and Villian was right, they needed to know exactly what they were dealing with. As much as he felt they needed to move, if something happened to him, secrets would be lost.

"Barakar is Raykan's twin brother."

Chapter 8 – Suntra

Queen Silvarna and General Bluewing flew to the sacred gem cave. The council were waiting for them to report on the worrying news delivered the day before. Silvarna had expected to make this journey only once with her mate, Pathanclaw, when they had finally been reunited on their home world of Arcus.

General Bluewing felt his new role keenly as Queen Silvarna followed him through the Suntra sky. The sun was rising on what he knew would be a long day, but he felt proud of the work he was achieving with the younglings. It amused him to think what Pathandon would say about him teaching younglings battle tactics. It only seemed like a small blink of an eye for a dragon, that Pathandon and the king had left and before this, they had been the ones in training. Now Pathandon was on another world and Bluewing was the general of their army. He couldn't help but long for those past days. He'd always strived to be the best, to make his family proud, always to be older than he needed. Now he regretted not embracing his youth, but it was too late now to change the path of his life.

Bluewing felt proud as he led Queen Silvarna to the gem cave. After many long hours, they landed in front of the cave and the guardian was ready to greet them. It was awe inspiring and more than any of them could have imagined. He saw Queen Silvarna's eyes widen at the sight. It was not for the living to know this place. It was a vision they should only witness before their death.

Knowing their death gave life and the power of magic to keep the dragons' legacy alive. It was not something to take back to the living world. It was a testament to the strange and worrying times that they were doing so now.

They flew through the caves, Queen Silvarna wondering what had made these giant holes. Surely not the lava fires? She would ask Pathanclaw when he returned, if he returned. Silvarna moved these negative thoughts away. It was her role to be strong, to be ready to leave when her mate and her grandson returned. Doubts had no place in her mind. The ache of so many lost was hard to bear, but it was replaced quickly if her mind desired it, by clinging to the hope of the female dragons returning. Would there be another red female for Pathandon? Had any of the others survived? Her mind stopped its questions as they reached inside the mountain. This place was making her melancholy.

Even though Bluewing was prepared, he was still shocked at the sight of the cavern. He couldn't comprehend how many dragons must have died to create this immense mountain of gems. His thoughts mirrored Silvarna's. The gems created a kaleidoscope across the walls where the moonlight reflected through tiny holes in the cavern roof. They landed on one of the many giant lips of solid rock which protruded into the cavern.

Longsong inclined her head over to the right and Bluewing and Silvarna could see why the guardians had been so concerned. The gems had turned grey, all the colour and power had been sucked from them somehow. One touch would probably turn them to dust.

"How could this be?" Queen Silvarna asked, shocked at such a sight amongst this colourful landscape.

"Something is draining the gems. This is normal process for the gems, as we use the magic the gems will gradually lose colour and fade. These are removed from the cave and they help form the worlds in other ways."

"What other ways?" Queen Silvarna asked. What did that mean for a dragon if all the gems were used? Were they also no more?

"They are no use to a dragon once all power has been removed from them. The magic we need from them is exhausted but they create what the humans call minerals. These power the earth, the planets and are precious to the humans on Arcus. They hold no magical power as we know it. But the humans mined these on Arcus, and to them, they have a value."

"How are they being drained? What is your theory?" Bluewing asked, keen to know, so they could come up with a plan.

Longsong nodded at his directness. *"I believe somehow, a human has found the way to harness this power through a dragon. Nothing else has consumed my thoughts since I uncovered the extent of the treachery. No dragon could drain these gems in such a way and so quickly, even accounting for the extra power King Pathanclaw, Battlewing and Pathandon used to travel through time."*

An ache touched Bluewing's heart.

"I am sorry for the loss of Battlewing, General Bluewing. He was a mighty warrior and he would have been a valuable asset to us here. But I believe King Pathanclaw would have made Pathandon consume his essence, so one day he will power our family once more."

Another ache, this time of gratitude and awe that a Green would address him in such a way. They were unknown due to their solitary existence in the caves, but the colour of family did not matter, they were all one.

"Thank you, Longsong, I am grateful for your words. Is there any way to stop this?" Bluewing decided he needed to keep the important matter at the fore.

"I could put a protection spell over the gems, but that would make them inaccessible to King Pathanclaw and

without the power, they cannot move through the portal without other means."

"You're right. That is not an option. We need to give them every chance to rescue the female dragons and return here before we make our way to Arcus."

Silvarna cleared her throat and Bluewing realised his mistake.

"Sorry, we all recognise and thank you for your great service for agreeing to stay behind. We all remain grateful and proud of the service you give, so we all may live and thrive."

Queen Silvarna felt as if General Battlewing was alive and well, and speaking through his son. He would be so proud. She must remember to tell his mother.

Longsong nodded, unconcerned at her sacrifice. "The option we do have is to channel the power so that I can converse with King Pathanclaw. If he is aware of the danger, there may be something he can do."

"That is possible?" General Bluewing asked, hoping they could learn the fate of the two remaining. All the dragons knew King Pathanclaw and Pathandon were alive, they would have felt the death as they did with his father, but were their kin safe? Had they found the females? This knowledge would help them. So much was unknown.

"Yes. It is complicated and it will inevitably use the energy of a great number of the gems but if we do not stop this destruction, then all is lost for your return to Arcus."

"Then there is no choice. Prepare as you need to. How long before you're ready and what do you need from us?"

"Queen Silvarna, I will need you to be the channel. You already have the strongest link with your mate, so it will make the process easier. But I must warn you, there are risks."

"What do you mean?" Bluewing asked. Queen Silvarna didn't need to know. She would do whatever it took.

"I don't know the damage this could cause by creating this link through time and across worlds. It has only been tried once when the dragons left Arcus and found their way to Suntra. The dragon who created this link did not survive."

"No. I will not risk you. The King asked me to keep you safe, I…" Bluewing stopped, already knowing the queen would do this deed, no matter the cost to her.

"It's okay, General Bluewing. I understand your concern but this must be done. The King and Pathandon need to be warned of this, there is no doubt."

Bluewing nodded, he knew it was the right thing to do. But how would he face the King and his friend if he failed to keep the Queen safe?

Queen Silvarna moved her head and touched his. "Be still, Bluewing. My husband knows my stubbornness is legendary. He would not blame you."

"It is settled. Come back here in two nights and we will be ready." Longsong bowed and led them out of the cavern.

Queen Silvarna couldn't help but stare at the scar of greying gems which ran through the cave. Would hers soon be here, joining the long line which had gone before her and without her mate as they planned?

Before they took flight, Ember stopped them. "There is something else you should know. When we left Arcus, we left more than just the cave behind. Others stayed with the guardians until we could return. They accepted the long sleep and the parting. Never expecting, but hoping to see our kind again. You must know this in case King Pathanclaw does not return. It was our secret to keep all these years. I didn't agree with it at the time, but it wasn't my secret to share until now. I hope it will help to know our kin are waiting for us."

Queen Silvarna and General Bluewing flew back in silence but their minds were alive with questions.

Chapter 9 – Arcus

Raykan looked at the book and then Baynard, trying to judge if he really was going to burn it. Surely, the king would want to keep such a treasure, despite Baynard threatening to burn everything and rid Arcus of magic. He would be foolish to destroy an object if he might gain an advantage from its existence.

The flame inched closer and closer to the precious book. Not everything was lost as long as Prince Villian still had the book the Keeper had entrusted to him. Who knew what perils he had encountered? Was he even still alive? But in his heart Raykan knew Prince Villian was alive. He had to be. The future depended on him. But doubts nagged like snakes in his mind, as they always did. Had he given the boy enough knowledge? Maybe he should have taught him more about magic. Something to help him. But Pathanclaw and he had made a pact all that time ago. Humans could not be trusted with knowledge like that. They didn't respect life enough until it was too late.

He pulled back and Baynard smiled, thinking he had the better of him. But the flame wasn't the reason. He was no fan of fire, but in truth he was tired. He'd endured so many lifetimes and seen so many men like Baynard come and go. If only humans could realise the gift of a long life was more grief than delight, more anguish than happiness.

He sighed and said, "Do what you will, Baynard. I am beyond caring and nothing your rotting, evil mind can do will change that. Burn the book, burn me, but you will go to hell along with me."

Baynard pulled back, as a glow emitted from the book. A few words had slotted into place. Not much more than a parlour trick but the book knew its own kind. A gold shimmer reached the corners of his dark cell, the light reflecting in the eyes of a rat as it scurried to find the welcome of the darkness.

The king's aide dropped the wick and it seemed to float, almost like a feather catching the currents of the fetid air in the cell, rising and falling. Baynard was transfixed by the sight. The wick landed as gently as a kiss on the stone floor and the flame died, leaving Baynard's mouth open and Raykan's lifted with a smile.

Baynard caught his prisoner's smile and kicked the book out into the corridor. Without another word, he left the cell, his petulant footsteps being replaced with the sounds of the other prisoner's screams. A guard filled the doorway and before pulling the door shut, he threw something to Raykan. The sound reverberated around his small prison.

Raykan stretched and picked up the cold, heavy key off the cobbled dank floor. He wondered if Lady Cartina had arranged this, or if the guard was loyal to Prince Villian; it was the same thing. He put the key in his pocket and lent back. Closing his eyes, he settled down to regain his strength. Soon, he would be ready to leave. He hoped the others would be ready too.

Lady Cartina folded the piece of parchment carefully and passed it to her maid. She was playing a dangerous game and she knew it. She smiled at Luciana who had been with her since her childhood, had perhaps shaped her more than her parents ever had. Her parents were kind people, even if her father was quick to anger and too keen to seek approval from the King. Villian's father needed their family's army and vice versa.

As the maid left to take her note, Lady Cartina waited anxiously in her room. Pacing the floor, she went to her bedside cupboard and carefully took out the letter Villian had given her before he'd left on his quest. She moved outside to the balcony and looked over the gardens where she and Villian had walked on that first night. Her cheeks blushed as she thought of that evening. It had gone by so quickly, like a dream, but it would be etched in her memory forever, unlike the wisps of a dreams.

She had been terrified on the night they'd met. Worried they wouldn't like each other after her parents had told her the importance of the match. Lady Cartina had the feeling her father had misled the king about the strength of their army. She knew her father felt this marriage would quell any possible rebellion. Despite the rumours about clashes between the different houses for years. But no-one would dare take on the might of King Palell. Everyone had also heard the rumours of his failing health and with his only son missing... there were power plays in the background. Whispers filled the corridors and secret meetings were taking place across the lands.

She sighed as she lent on the cold stone balcony and her fingers worried the ring, hoping the one she had given to her prince was giving as much comfort. The ring felt warm as she twisted it, thinking of him doing the same. Her grandfather's rings were special, he'd told her that they were to mark a relationship which would bind them through life, time and past death. As soon as she'd seen her prince, she had known he would be the only one worthy of this gift. They'd had so little time before her betrothed had left. She couldn't believe how great her feelings were for him.

It was some time before the door to her chambers

opened and her maid returned, joining her on the balcony. They grasped hands as Lady Cartina waited for the answer.

"All is well my lady. The meeting has been arranged. They will meet you after dark at the agreed place."

"Thank you, my loyal friend. I know what I ask of you and the risks you take."

"My lady, I would give my life for you. My loyalty has always been with you."

"So, nothing to do with a rather large Smithy then?" Lady Cartina teased.

Her maid blushed, and it warmed Lady Cartina's heart to see her feel so much. She didn't believe her closest maid could not have a relationship. How could she deny them the feelings she had for Prince Villian? Feelings were not only for the young or privileged. She could tell Luciana had changed when she'd returned from her first clandestine meeting with Ironhand and the Keeper of Books after Morbark had made contact with Luciana. Lady Cartina felt honoured that his friends had turned to her and she would do justice to their trust.

"Let us speak no more on this. We do not know who is listening and these are dangerous times. We need to be patient and until then, everything must go on as normal. I have an audience with the King very soon. I must be ready."

Luciana nodded, "I will get your gown ready my lady."

Lady Cartina looked after her maid and her smile faded. Could she really put her close friends at risk? If she were caught, it wouldn't only be her that would suffer; Luciana, her mother, father and even though she didn't like her sister, Helendy was still family. She would have to be careful. She put Villian's letter away and perched on the end of the bed. She twisted the ring again, feeling the metal warm as she turned it repeatedly. Could she really make a difference? Her grandfather had always been full of stories her father didn't approve of, but she had lapped them up as a child and now, here she was, a lady about to marry a Prince who was on a quest to bring back the dragons. Her maid had heard the rumours as she quietly walked the streets, listening and learning. It seemed like one of the fairy tales her sister so often talked about. Her sister had been furious when she learned she wouldn't be the one to marry the prince...

"Are you ready, my lady?"

Lady Cartina's hand dropped. She stood up straight and went to put on her armour, even if it was an embroidered gold dress. She had chosen her path, and she would do everything in her power to make sure that when Villian returned, he would find his friends and allies waiting for him.

Chapter 10 – Luminosa

Star came out of her daydream feeling groggy. Instantly a feeling of dread overtook her as she knew someone had used magic on her. The Master's had been trying to steal her memories, like they did when they arrived on Luminosa for the first time. A roar from Dragon had woken her, shaken her from this un-natural remembrance. They wanted to know what she knew. She wouldn't let them do it. Had she already revealed too much?

She cleared her head and formed a plan. She needed to get away. They had searched her. Triana must have told them she had a weapon. Looking around she saw a sharp rock protruding through the side of the natural rock prison. She shuffled over and began working the rope that bound her hands. There were no guards here. If the children escaped, where would they escape to? Beyond the woods, there was only desert. But she had friends, and she would get out and make the Masters and Triana pay. Would Galan respond to her? Would he help them? She knew he always talked of escaping. If they worked together, then maybe they would have a chance.

The last thread finally gave way. She was sweating and dusty as she rubbed her hands together. They were sore and bleeding but she didn't care about that. Now to get Dragon free. She heard a noise and pushed herself to back of the cage, pushed her arms behind her and locked her hands together. Her breath was coming fast and she made an effort to slow it down. She had to look defeated.

Triana appeared before her and it was all Star could do not to rush over and grab her by the neck. The pain of her nails digging into her hands kept her still.

"I've brought you some water and food."

Star glared at her.

"Well, that's rude. I didn't have to you know. I could have left you here to rot with your stupid Dragon." Triana sighed, "Have it your own way." She kicked over the water so it soaked into the food ball.

Dragon made a noise and Triana turned to the cage. "Not so fearsome now, are you? Thinking you could come back here and beat the Masters, just like that." Triana clicked her fingers. "A few months' training and you thought you could win!"

Triana laughed, and Star had never wanted to put her new muscles to such good use. Her whole being ached to launch at her, but not yet.

"Why are you helping them, Triana? What have they ever done for you? The dragons could have burnt you alive but they let you live. Why have you done this?"

"The dragons are dying out, Star. Without the females here, one day the dragons will be no more. Well, not their kind anyway. The magical ones are the future. The dragons want to keep it all for themselves. They don't want mere humans to have magic. They want to control us."

"Don't be stupid, Triana. It's the Masters who are controlling us and stealing us from our parents and keeping us here, not the dragons. The dragons want to live in peace, like we all do."

"Don't be such a baby, Star. The dragons are the ones who caused this mess. They only shared it with a human by mistake and then they ruined everything when they tried to take it back from us. We deserve the power as much as they do."

"What are you talking about, Triana? How do you know so much?"

Triana didn't reply, perhaps realising she had said too much. Star wondered if she was telling the truth. Did Pathanclaw have more secrets he wasn't sharing with them? Could they really trust the dragons? Did they only want to use them to get to Arcus and kill all the other humans? She looked over to Dragon. Despite hers being magical, she wouldn't believe the dragons were bad. They didn't have to keep them all alive Villian was the one they had been waiting for all these years. Pathanclaw and Pathandon could have just killed them and taken him. No, Triana was lying.

Triana looked towards the entrance to the prison within the cave. Maybe there was a guard? That could be a problem. Star needed to find out more.

"How is everyone? Please tell me they are alright? You spent months with us on that world, Triana. I don't know why you're being like this. We have a chance to escape and do what we want. No longer controlled by the Masters. Why would you try and stop us?"

Star wanted to keep her talking to try and distract her so she could plan her escape. If Triana came close enough she could grab her and make her open the cell.

"US. US," Triana spat the words out, "because US, does not include me! It never has. You and your pathetic friends. I would never have been part of that."

"That's your fault," Star shouted back, "we tried to like you and forgive you for being an evil piece of dragon dung but you wouldn't let us. You are nasty through and through."

In her anger Star stood up and stepped forward, forgetting she was supposed to be pretending to have her hands tied. She gripped the bars on the cell, as Triana took a step back.

A slow smile, turned into a grin, "Well, they cannot say it was my fault, you were trying to escape."

Triana lifted her hand and started mumbling magic

words. Star looked in horror as a glow began to emit from Triana's hands. She was conjuring a fire ball.

Chapter 11 – Suntra

Bluewing looked to the elders. The Silver Dragon of Argarnax and Mercery. Silver now alone after his mate Saydn died or was lost when they escaped Arcus. Maybe she was still alive on Arcus. The news from the guardians brought fresh hope. Only Venthrax of the Gold elders had made the long voyage to Suntra. Vorbex and Hatalon were now the nominated elders since arriving on Suntra. Bluewing should have had hundreds of years in human time to learn this role and earn the respect of the elders, before being nominated. But he was determined he would make everyone proud. He would be the protector they needed. He would lead them to safety and keep them together. He'd expected some of the younglings to be a problem but even they realised the seriousness of their situation. The day their king had left, they had all grown, and once they'd taken the step of responsibility, there was no going back.

It had been a meeting which bore no good news, so it was with a heavy heart as they informed the council of the new developments. It wasn't only Raykan who was weary of a long life. The Elders had seen so much, even they felt weary of time and its demands.

The elders had finally nodded their agreement and they parted, all lost in their worries about the disappearance of the gems, but with hope, they could be reunited with their kin on Arcus. Questions about the truth surrounding the dragons becoming allergic to humans were forefront in the discussions. How could it be that the dragons had stayed to protect the gem cave on Arcus if this were true? But why would King Pathanclaw have lied? Silvarna had defended him but deep down she'd known he'd been hiding something all these years. It wasn't just the worry of their future which haunted his dreams and waking eye. She'd never asked. Maybe because she hadn't wanted to know.

When Pathanclaw had mentioned returning to Arcus, he'd said that surely enough time had passed for whatever ailed the dragons who were in contact with humans to have passed. Or maybe they could find a way to reverse it? They believed they had killed the human responsible, maybe this problem had died with him? Maybe. So many questions she needed answers to. With the power of the guardians, she would speak to her beloved in a few days. But the guardians had warned her of the dangers, she couldn't keep the connection for long with Pathanclaw, even if they managed it. The dire warning of death was present in her mind. She would do it, no matter the consequences, but what if she died? Right there in the cave. She supposed it would make the guardians job easier and she smiled. Her son, Pathandon's father would have smiled, his dark humour matching hers. He and his wife had been gone. So long. Even if she did die, she would not be alone. But it was always a dragon's hope to end their gift of life and be together in death.

She flew to find Kyanite. She was, of course, still feeling the loss of her mate Battlewing, as she would until her time came. Silvarna wanted to tell her of all the brave deeds her son was performing and how proud she was. They would fly through the skies of Suntra, and she hoped it wasn't for the last time.

Chapter 12 – Arcus

It was time for the plans to come to fruition. Lady Cartina moved between the shadows of the trees with her heart in her mouth. She decided she wasn't as brave as she imagined Villian would be. Every single noise terrified her and the sounds of the night creatures made her conjure up images of monsters. She could imagine them jumping out from behind a tree with their large, bloodied teeth, ready to devour their next meal.

A figure emerged from behind the tree and a hand quickly covered her mouth, managing to muffle the rest of her scream. She felt breath tickle her neck, as words reached her ears.

"It's alright my Lady. It's Dyana. You are safe."

The hand left her mouth and Lady Cartina tried to inhale quietly to slow her heart. She turned to look up at the tall woman who led Prince Villian's warriors. The fiercest of them all, but her touch and voice were as gentle as any lady in the great halls.

Lady Cartina had witnessed their fighting and was in awe of their strength and beauty when they trained in the courtyard. All twelve of Prince Villian's warriors were ferocious with their long braided hair which had been tied back to avoid the enemy getting a purchase and gaining an advantage. They were all tanned and toned. Every one of them, a skilled horsewoman and fighter. Lady Cartina had had doubts about Prince Villian's choice in a wife. She was none of these things, her pale skin a reflection not only of her mother but of being kept inside to do lady-like tasks. Staring at these brave warriors she vowed to make her beloved proud – she would also be a fierce warrior.

"Come, my lady. The others are waiting for us."

Dyana led her through some dense woodland and Lady Cartina wondered how she could see a path. She could see nothing and had to keep close to avoid tripping over. Animal noises came through the dark night, signals from the other warriors. They would not make the mistake Raykan had made the night Villian left. If anyone dared to follow them, they would soon find themselves staring sightless into a moonless sky.

Finally, they arrived at the edge of the dense woodland which gave way to a shocking black wasteland. She knew this had been created when the virus took hold and hundreds of dragons were scorched to the earth. Lady Cartina shuddered at the thought of so many dragons being killed on this spot. She knew some of the old stories from her grandfather, and since being in the castle she had borrowed many books before the king had ordered the library to be cleared and the books burned. She knew the Keeper had employed some of the light-fingered children to acquire as many as the old books as they could. She herself had more than a few hidden in her chambers.

Lady Cartina moved into the clearing. It was easy to see Ironhand – his large frame unmistakeable. He reached over and enveloped her, like a bear hugging a squirrel. She could still smell the forge upon him, even though he'd been in hiding in the forest since Prince Villian had left. She smiled as he let her go, his touch so gentle. She could see why Villian trusted this great bear of a man and could she why her maid Luciana blushed. He had a sparkle in his eye and mirth was never far. The Keeper of Books nodded at her. In contrast she would find it most awkward if he hugged her but she welcomed his quiet strength and, as Villian trusted him, that was good enough for her.

The four of them waited until the signals assured them they were safe. They had not been followed.

"My lady," the Keeper of Books began, "it is good to have you on our side. What can you tell us about, Raykan?"

"He is well, erm, Keeper," she stumbled on his name. Did everyone call him Keeper of Books?

He saved her blushes, "Please, my lady. Call me Valivar."

Lady Cartina could see Ironhand looked shocked. Maybe he'd never heard the Keepers name before either. She nodded and continued, "I have visited him and we are to meet him here in two days' time. He seemed very weak, but confident that he would be able to escape and meet us here. One of the guards should have given him a key and hopefully he will be able to slip out without anyone noticing."

"We are incredibly grateful that you risked your life. It was a brave thing to do, my lady."

Lady Cartina blushed at the compliment from Valivar.

"We need to be ready to leave. Dyana will the ship be ready for us?" Valivar asked as he turned to the warrior.

Dyana stepped closer to the group, her eyes had been scanning the forest, her attention half on the conversation while listening for signals of any danger which lay in the woods.

"Yes, I've spoken to the captain and he was most obliging. They will be ready and waiting in the bay. He said he's keen to stretch her legs."

Lady Cartina gasped at this until Dyana clarified saying he meant the ship. All captains called their ships she, despite his ship having a giant figure of a dragon on the front.

Ironhand just managed to turn a chuckle into a cough,

as Lady Cartina couldn't help a small nervous laugh escape into the air. They both quietened at a 'shh' from Valivar, and her eyes met Ironhand's as they smiled at their rebuke. There was nothing more guaranteed in life to quieten you than a command from a Librarian.

"Good," Valivar said, "I suggest we meet back here in two days' time then and we ensure we are ready to leave. Lady Cartina, you will have to take great care whilst we are away. Do not do anything to draw interest from any quarter. When Raykan escapes they will be looking for someone to blame."

"But, I'm coming with you. That was the plan? I cannot stay here as Villian's friends need my help."

"My Lady, you will be more help to us in the castle. There is no-one we can trust more than you to keep us informed. It will give us more information than we could have ever have hoped for without your help."

Lady Cartina felt slightly better, but she didn't like the thought of everyone leaving her alone in the castle with only her maid. What would happen when Villian returned or if they found out she had helped Raykan? What if Baynard tortured the guards and they gave her away? What then? What about her family?

"We will not leave you completely unguarded. Rest assured, many of the castle guards are loyal to Villian's cause and have vowed to protect you and your maid. Should you find yourself in need of escape then send your maid to the forge and Ironhand's apprentice will help you get away."

"It's time to leave," Dyana said. "It's not wise to spend too long here."

Ironhand enveloped her again and whispered, "Stay safe my lady." The Keeper of Books nodded and turned to leave. It seemed they had decided her fate. Lady Cartina followed Dyana until they were back at the tree, from here she knew her way back into the castle.

"Be safe, my lady. It is an honour to serve you. My life and the lives of my warriors are yours."

She didn't know what to say to this, but settled with, "Thank you, Dyana. It is an honour to have your protection."

This seemed acceptable and the warrior nodded and blended into the background. Dyana was so different to her sister. Luciana had told her, Dyana and Lanu had lost a sister when they were younger. It might explain why Lady Cartina always felt protected by them, it wasn't just because they were warriors. A few signals marked the end of this exciting evening. Lady Cartina took a deep breath and made her way back to the castle, her thoughts once again turning to her betrothed. She could see why men wanted adventure. She had never felt so alive.

Enough time had passed and Raykan was ready to leave. His energy was back and he could once again join the words in his mind. He remembered the time he'd tried to explain it to his twin brother, how the magic was there, the words were in his mind but they were jumbled. Like a letter which had been torn into shreds and had to be painstakingly fitted together, but he turned from thoughts of his long dead twin brother, or the brother he hoped was dead. He swallowed his feelings deep inside.

He'd been surprised he'd been left alone. Baynard had not returned and he hadn't been dragged out and tortured. Time had passed in solitude, healing and reflection. Time. He hoped the others were ready. Making him worry. Something wasn't right, he would have to proceed with caution. He hoped that Lady Cartina could do her part and his friends would be waiting. This was not something he could do alone. He focused on the future, in which he could see Prince Villian and Lady Cartina on the throne. They would bring Arcus back to the peace of the past, his old friend Pathanclaw and Silvarna ruling alongside, their enemies beaten and the mistakes of the past never repeated.

He understood why Pathanclaw had been reluctant to teach him magic, he knew now, it should never have come to pass. Humans were not worthy. Even with his knowledge and wisdom, the feeling of power was addictive, the magic thrummed through his body, making him more than he was. He felt at one with the world, as if the whole universe was at his fingertips. It was the most dangerous feeling, even stronger than the power and influence of a king. The only thing he was grateful for was that the magic was short lived. If he didn't need to rest after using the magic he knew he would have already lost himself. He wasn't sure he would be able to stop himself wanting more.

He closed his eyes and formed the words. He touched the shackles securing him to wall. They glowed before splitting and setting his body free. He took a moment to lay them carefully to avoid any undue noise. He wanted to leave quietly. He listened for a moment and tried the key the guard had left; it turned easily in the lock. He held his breath but the sound of a scream made him wince. He felt guilty for leaving these poor people to their fate, but he needed to leave without detection. He didn't want to lead danger to his friends.

Raykan pulled his hood over his head and moved quietly. He had been in this prison once before and his burns seem to ache at this memory. He moved further, careful with his steps as he didn't have his staff to take the strain and pain out of walking. He moved towards the exit as the ground gradually sloped upwards as if encouraging the walker to pick up the pace and finally to feel the coolness which awaited outside, to breathe clean air once again. His lungs needed it as much as his body needed food or water. A sound ahead made him pause. The footsteps were heading his way. He looked around and could see nowhere to hide. He'd hoped to leave quietly, but now he had little choice as the footsteps moved closer.

Chapter 13 – Luminosa

Villian couldn't believe what he was hearing. Barakar was Raykan's twin brother!

"But why didn't Raykan tell me this? He must know that to win this war the Masters have to be killed, and this includes his brother!"

"Raykan is ashamed of who his brother has become, as am I, and we will never forgive ourselves for what we did. What we are still doing to the worlds. We truly believed, no, I must tell the truth, we convinced ourselves he'd been killed on Arcus. Believe me when I say we have punished ourselves more than anyone could. I did not want to take on this responsibility, I wanted to stay on Arcus and face the consequences, but the council forced me to leave. It was their last wish. They foretold the future. The council could see 'the one' would come and that we would once again be able to live amongst humans. They believed enough time would pass for it to be safe or we would find a cure for the virus which drove us away." Pathanclaw paused and looked at Prince Villian.

Pol moved close and put their hand on King Pathanclaw's on the patch where his scales were missing. Pathanclaw sighed. As the deep breath left him, he turned his giant head and the tiny form of Pol placed theirs against his and time seemed to pause.

Prince Villian didn't want to break this up, but he was impatient to move now they knew more. A part of him wished he hadn't asked. If he were face to face with Barakar, would he be able to kill him, knowing it was

Raykan's brother? No matter what the consequence would be if he let him live? The Masters had to be stopped. He would have to do it if it came to it. Could he beat someone who had been honing his magic kills for thousands of years? How was that even possible? How much power did Barakar really have? Always so many questions with the answers unknown.

Finally, Pol moved away and went to sit on a rock.

Pathanclaw continued, *"It was my fault for teaching Raykan and he in turn shared my shame by teaching his brother. I would argue we were naive, but I should have known better. I failed my kin, embarrassed my family name."*

Pathanclaw turned to his grandson, *"I've wanted to tell you so many times that it was I who brought our fate upon us. But shame and regret are powerful. I thought by leaving and putting it right, I would one day afford myself some redemption. But the more I see how my folly has affected so many; no, I don't think forgiveness is mine to expect or demand."*

"You are wrong, Grandfather. I have not known humans long, especially compared to our measure of time, but I know that our kin and theirs have great forgiveness in their hearts. We all make mistakes. Maybe this was meant to happen. Our stories tell us of many terrible times in the past which were all part of a bigger plan which couldn't have been foreseen until the journey was over."

"Grandson, when did you become so wise?" Pathanclaw asked with pride.

"I learnt everything I know from you, Grandfather. I am proud to be your grandson and I'm proud that you are my King. None will say otherwise. They will forgive the past. We will forgive the past. We do not need to keep secrets. Not anymore."

Silence again overtook them, as they all thought about what they had lost and gained in their lives. So many threads, so many choices had all led to this moment. What other moments would there be where they could not see the path they were on. What choices would they make on the long journey ahead which would no doubt cause pain but hopefully end in peace? Was one life worth more than another to make it come to pass?

"We must move." Prince Villian's words brought them back from their melancholy thoughts.

"Yes. We must," Pathanclaw answered, a new lightness in his voice, relieved he had finally started to share his burden and grateful for their forgiveness even though he knew he did not deserve it.

Thanan hugged Pol before moving towards Pathandon. His head bent low to allow Thanan to climb onto his back more easily. Prince Villian nodded at Pol and then climbed onto Pathanclaw. Villian noticed a fleeting change in Pol, as quick as a flash the purple he'd seen in their eyes was back to the dark orange he was used to.

'Okay, Pol. I will let you know when we reach the other end.'

'Be safe my friends.' Pol walked out of the oasis as the dragons rose silently into the air. Pol moved through the corridor, they had something they needed to do first.

Chapter 14 – Suntra

Kyanite and Silvarna finally settled on the mountainside. Not too long ago she had waited for the dawn with Pathanclaw, wondering what the future held.

"How long have you known?"

Queen Silvarna knew the question would be asked. She had known, but thought it was impossible. Had felt the knowledge of it when she had agreed to speak to Pathanclaw and put her life in danger. A stirring she had tried to ignore, but it could be dismissed no longer.

Queen Silvarna turned, the rising dawn casting red flames across the landscape. The start of a new day. Dragons believed each new day brought promise and opportunity. The chance to be with a friend or loved one, to just be. She turned to a friend she had known since they were younglings.

"For certain, yesterday. But maybe longer."

Kyanite sighed, *"It is a gift my Queen. We must tell the others."*

"No," Queen Silvarna answered more sharply than she intended. *"Sorry, no, no-one must know. Not now. Not until after."*

"But, my Queen, a life is precious. The Elders will not allow you to do this deed now. It must be another."

"If I must command you to be silent, I will. Please, Kyanite, don't make me do that. Not to you. I have not taken this decision lightly, but King Pathanclaw needs to know the situation with the gems."

"But someone else could do it?"

"The guardians said it needs to be someone close to him. No, please. You will not change my mind. It is how it has to be. No matter we are family, you know it can only be me."

Kyanite was quiet as they watched the sun rise higher in the sky. Finally, she answered, "I hope we do not live to regret this, my Queen."

Queen Silvarna nodded. She hoped so too. A new life was a precious gift but now. Why had this happened now?

Chapter 15 – Arcus

Laughter filled the corridor, an unusual sound in a dungeon, but the men who governed these dark depths were comfortable with pain and torture and took pleasure in the giving of it. There were two of them. Raykan would have to do something before he was spotted. He'd hoped he wouldn't have to use too much magic to leave the dungeon. Who knew what dangers he would face when he left and he would still need precious time to recuperate. He dreaded to think what a human could do with the unlimited access to magic. Once again, he steered his thoughts away from his brother.

Raykan concentrated on the spell he wanted to conquer. As he concentrated, he listened to the guards. They were shuffling around, an odd thing to do. They were mock fighting he realised, their footsteps going back and forth on the stone steps. Laughing as they hit each other.

"Oi, be careful. That bloody thing's sharp. You're going take my eye out."

"I will gut you like that spying peasant last week."

They both laughed.

"I wonder if this thing can do magic? Did you hear where Baynard said they found it? With that scarred monster from the depths of the forest. He gives me the creeps. Not a chance I'm going into his cell."

"Don't be a fool. Everyone knows magic is a myth. This isn't nothing but a lump of wood. Here I will show you."

The man banged it on the floor. It sounded like stone

hitting stone, rather than wood hitting a solid floor. The silence gave Raykan the precious moments he needed. He could imagine their shocked faces. He bent down and scraped up a handful of filthy gritty muck from the flagstones. He dreaded to think what it comprised of, but it would have to do. He would treat them to a little show.

Finally, he heard them move again. They were louder now, no doubt using this to mask their fear. They turned the corner still mock fighting with his staff, the other had a shield which they had no doubt stolen from another prisoner. The noise of the clash reverberated around the small space as Raykan stepped out into the middle of the corridor and waited for them to notice him. It didn't take long.

"Oi, you. What you doing out of your cell? You're going to pay, old man."

The guard with the shield set it against the wall. As he went to draw this sword, Raykan lifted his hand and blew the contents in their direction, whilst muttering the required words. The guards were transfixed as the small grains separated and swirled around. Raykan added a bit of colour for effect and soon they were enveloped in a maelstrom of rocks. On each rotation they became larger and larger. The first guard, mouth open, didn't get his hand up in time and was struck on the head, sending him unconscious to the floor. The other swung the staff around but there was little room and it bounced off the walls. Moments later, he joined his friend on the floor and the staff clattered to the ground.

"Oi, what are you two idiots doing down there? I've told you about messing about. If Baynard comes down here, he will have your heads. Now pack it in. I'm off for my break, do your rounds and get back here."

Raykan froze, but no-one was coming. He bent down and picked up his staff. It felt good to have it back in his hands. He could feel the power of the object. It gave him more than just an anchor to the ground and supported his painful body. He bent down and touched them both on the head. Their memories of what had happened would be unclear when they woke.

He paused a moment, and decision made, he took a set of keys off one of the guards and pushed them through the nearest cell window hole. Most were in a wretched state, but at least he had given them a chance. He had to get out.

"Please, do not escape yet. Wait for the signal. You will know it when it comes." Raykan said to the darkness. A pale, bloodied hand reached out and took the keys.

'We are with you,' came the scratchy voice, worn from screaming no doubt.

Raykan nodded and turned to leave. Just before reaching the exit to the prison, he turned right and moved down a corridor until he reached the place he was looking for. Set into the floor was the channel which let the waste out of the prison, into the river and finally the sea. He cast his last spell, aware his powers were draining. He held his breath, before lifting the grate and dropping into the fetid darkness.

The captain waited in the bay. He could smell the danger in the air. Sal had chosen his crew carefully. He knew the ones loyal to Prince Villian and his cause. Despite only being a boy, the prince had a loyal following. If they didn't believe the old tales of dragons and humans, somewhere deep inside they wanted to believe. Even a warrior secretly wanted peace, wanted to live their time with their families and not be wrenched away to fight someone else's war. If history were to be believed, peace had reigned for thousands of years, and people were bone weary of the wars that had followed. What did they have to lose?

The captain had set sail after the ship had been revealed to Arcus, a maiden voyage to test her out so their departure was not seen as unusual. He would pick the others up in the bay and they would wait on one of his secret islands until the signal came. He had over half the fleet on his side, but they were to remain behind to stop the rest of the fleet with the minimum force possible if it was needed. If this didn't go to plan, the battle would be messy. Despite the ruthlessness of the King, many followed him without question, not wanting the wrath of Baynard focused on them.

He'd heard Baynard had been mortally wounded on the night Prince Villian had left. The captain still shook his head at the thought of this young prince moving through time and to another place, another world. He'd stared at the night sky many a time wondering about life. Wondering what the stars were and if there was someone like him, looking down also wondering. It was more than a simple seafarer could stand. But he'd heard it straight from Ironhand's mouth and who wouldn't believe him; straight as they came and as loyal as a dog. But there was a different dog called Baynard who had somehow survived a fatal wound. It made him wonder what forces were at work.

It was because of Ironhand that Prince Villian had so many people willing to follow him. No-one would doubt the smith's intentions or his honour. Well, not without his giant shovel hands squeezing your neck. It had happened to him a few times when they had spent the night drinking the ale house dry; thankfully for him it had been in jest.

The evening was kind and a gentle breeze moved the sails quietly and calmly. He looked to the dragon head leading the way and puffed out his chest. This was the finest ship ever to grace the waters of Arcus. One day he might meet the real thing, a dragon. To behold a vision in his lifetime, he would gracefully sink with the ship and consider himself blessed.

There was a call in the night as they neared their mooring, and the signal was given. The guests he would welcome on board and take to safety. But had they all made it? He stared anxiously into the darkness as they lowered the small boat to row to shore.

"Lady Cartina. The King would like a word if you please."

She froze and set a smile on her face before turning to Baynard.

"Why, Sir Baynard. You made me jump."

"I am no Sir, my Lady."

Of course, she knew this, but it didn't do him any harm to be reminded. She considered that a victory for her betrothed.

"So soon? But I only spoke with the King yesterday." She placed her hands together in front of her gold gown and touched the ring, taking strength from it.

Lady Cartina and her maid needed to leave soon if they were to make the rendezvous in time. She knew The Keeper wanted her to stay in the castle, but as the hours passed, she felt herself in more and more danger. Her maid had heard worrying rumours. She had no-one to receive council from, to check if she was doing the right thing. She couldn't risk speaking to Dyana or seeking out Ironhand or The Keeper. She alone would have to make the decision and she had. Despite the danger to herself and the others, she had to leave. She knew in her heart it was not safe for her here anymore.

"Well, the King doesn't spare me to collect just anyone, my lady."

The way he said my lady, irked her. She knew he was being facetious, but it wouldn't be wise to challenge him.

She had also heard the rumours about his supposed resurrection from death.

"I completely understand. I am at the Kings disposal. As always." She nodded and walked ahead of him, towards the throne room, smiling to herself when he had to walk quickly to catch her. Her maid smiled as she fell into step behind her.

The feeling of dread built in Lady Cartina's stomach as she walked towards the throne room. What if the king had found out what she was doing? They had been so careful, but there was always someone willing to turn you in for the price of some coin. Her hand went to her stomach as she tried to quell her nerves. Her maid reached over and squeezed her hand quickly. Lady Cartina felt better. They had been careful; it would be okay.

Baynard had caught them up and with a nod, the guards opened the great doors to the throne room. It seemed strange to be entering this cavernous room without it being filled with noise and people. The King was on the throne, guards standing behind him and to the side. Her mother and father were waiting for her. Her stomach dropped, why would they be here? As she moved down the hall, their footsteps reverberating around the empty hall, a figure moved into sight from behind one of the pillars and joined her parents. Helendy! Lady Cartina almost said her name aloud. Her sister had that look on her face which spelt trouble for those around her.

POL

P ol moved through the cave after they had watched the others leave. Their friends were so brave, it made their heart sing. Pol knew they wouldn't be able to save them all. It was beyond their powers to stop the natural order of nature. Death belonged as much as life on the worlds, but still, sadness filled their heart.

Good people were as likely to die as bad. It was a part of the chaos of the cycle and it was better not to try and understand, even though most humans strived for understanding of their place.

Pol's mind opened and they explored the others. In Star's they felt only pain and sadness, with always a touch of fierceness, which made Pol smile. Pol did not tell them they could still hear Star. It was not their path to save her. Villian was full of determination and great deeds. Thanan's mind was filled with worry and hope. Pol smiled for their friend, Thanan, who had the purest heart of any creature they had ever encountered.

Pol walked as gently as the wind caressing a leaf on a warm day when Spring had started and the smells of the forest tickled Pol's nostrils. Pol longed for the forest, to feel nature and time.

Pol reached out and lightly touched the cave, feeling bad about desiring the forest over the cave. These were formed from a fire which had long since cooled and settled to the land. It had grown and blown its final fury on the world and formed the typography of the universe. They were the first shapers, then the worms, then the insects, the mammals, the dragons and now humans shaped the great worlds. What would be next? The cold made their body shiver.

They should not have been. They were a paradox of nature, humans were not in the great plan of the worlds. But despite the odds, here they were, shaping the worlds as the fires of the volcanos. As did time and weather. When humans emerged one day, it was thought they wouldn't last the seasons due to the harshness of the lands. The humans surprised all and so they'd been allowed. It wasn't right to go against the natural order of things. It was a mistake, one which the worlds were paying for, or maybe the reason would become clear. Good things could come of great tragedies.

How could they choose to end the humans now? They were capable of so much and yet continually let themselves and each other down. Pol had been sent to watch and learn, to decide the humans' fate once and for all. Maybe even the dragons, their impact was now felt across time, had changed worlds and the potential for so much, but would it be death and destruction or peace?

This had been an impossible task. The Masters were evil, but they were no worse than the fungus that covered a tree until it suffocated. Were they worse than the birds which preyed on other creatures and ate their young? Maybe the difference could be to argue that most creatures did these deeds for survival; not rage, not jealousy, their own gain, spite, or mercy, but to survive. Others followed the natural order.

Pol ran their hand over the cold wall again, feeling the time pass. Maybe they should leave now and let fate decide the path of these complicated creatures who were not meant to be. But Pol kept walking, moving to the mouth of the cave entrance so they could be in the right place when Thanan, Villian and Star needed their friend. It was important to do what they had agreed. To keep watching and observing.

Despite their worry and fear, Thanan and Star had pulled through. They needed protection and so Pol had made sure they were okay no matter the cost to them. Pol had interfered more than was allowed. Too many times Pol had ached when it was not their place to change and influence. More and more they understood the emotions which drove the humans to act on something instinctively and without thought to consequence. It seemed the longer Pol spent in their company the more their actions mirrored their friends.

The day Star and Pol had come across the other dragons, Pol had never known such anger. It had thrummed through their body; they had felt like they could split the world in half with just a thought. Maybe they had that power but to use it was unthinkable.

A tremor no-one else would be able to detect held Pol's attention. They stopped in the cold, dark, lava created corridor, waiting to see what the world had to tell. Was it grumbling at its mistreatment, or giving a warning? Were the great fires building from below? The planets were not unfeeling, solid objects as humans thought. They raged their wars and expected no consequence. The worlds lived and breathed. They danced their slow graceful arch through time, which had no meaning to them. Not that any human could understand.

Pol continued walking, it was just a grumble, like a youngling when they were coming into their power and didn't know what to do with it. Like a human young who couldn't control themselves until they settled into themselves, finding peace – well some did.

Pol had nearly reached the large training cave where Thanan and the other children learned their magic, as should not be in the natural order of things. How had the Masters found this planet? Were they betrayed? It wasn't the worm's fault that they shared such knowledge. They had seen more moons than could be counted and were here long before humans arrived this place, which was as awe inspiring as it was dangerous. Humans may have called them Gods. They meddled but who could stop them? Would they be any better than humans if they interfered? Could they see the bigger plan. Was it arrogance to think they were superior?

The air changed as Pol left the snug corridors of the cave and stepped into the expanse where the worms lived. As Pol moved towards the middle of the cave, they heard Thanan in their mind. Pol smiled. His gentle, young voice, so full of fear for his friend. Excitement at his adventure and need to make Villian proud made Pol realise the humans would be left to see out their cycle. It was not for them to decide their fate. Time would decide, as it always had. Maybe it was time.

After Pol had assured Thanan they were ready, Pol moved to the middle of the great cave and floated to the top of the cave. As they reached the top, they slowed down. Moments later the familiar voice entered their mind. A voice they had not heard and thought they never would again.

"Welcome back, Pol."

Tobias's quiet tones soothed Pol's worries. It felt like coming home.

Chapter 16 – Luminosa

The dragons dropped Villian and Thanan as close to their new quest as they could. Villian had thought about asking if Pol was strong enough to pull the children through, but Pol had given him a look before he'd voiced it and he'd kept it to himself. Pol was a puzzle to him. He couldn't work out how they could have so much power but wouldn't use it against anyone. He understood the power to protect but sometimes people had to get hurt to fix things for everyone. Maybe there was another way, but it was a way which was closed to him.

Villian and Thanan drew their weapons, but they knew they wouldn't be much use against the Masters. Thanan's magic might help them for a time, but he knew he was no Master. Thanan would be best to divert their attention with a fireball and run away if it came to a straight out fight with them. The dragons circled for a while before moving off to search for the females. Thanan could tell Pathanclaw was desperate to free them after all this time without them. He now knew the stronger urge Pathanclaw had to set things right. The female dragons were important if the dragons were to thrive. Even after this short time, Thanan couldn't imagine a world without dragons. He couldn't find the anger within to blame Pathanclaw for his part in how his future had been shaped.

As they moved through the woods towards the cave, Thanan wondered how Star was fairing. He tried to reach out for her but worryingly he still couldn't hear her. He didn't know what he would do if she and Dragon were dead. A great wave of anger swept over him, and he nearly dropped to the floor. He clenched his fists; magic was coursing through his body. Villian reach out to touch him and jumped back as a lightning shock surged through his fingers.

"Thanan." He sounded scared.

Thanan held his hand up, "It's okay. I'm okay. Sorry."

"What was that?"

"I don't know. I've never felt like that before. The magic, it took me over somehow. I couldn't control it."

This silenced them both. If he couldn't learn to control his magic, it put them all in danger.

"Are you sure you're, okay?"

"Yes, come on, let's go."

Villian reached out his hand, despite the risk of a shock and he pulled Thanan from the ground. Thanan dusted the dirt off his clothes, and they continued quietly through the woods, both wondering what this meant. For Thanan it seemed strange to be walking back through this familiar landscape as an intruder. For so long, he had belonged here, had a right to be here, even if he was always desperate to get away. Maybe they should have stayed where they were and waited to see where the Masters took them.

"Speed up a bit," Villain whispered.

Thanan hadn't realised his thoughts had slowed him down and he picked up the pace. They were nearly at the cave entrance. He motioned to Villian, and he moved to the front with his sword held, ready for battle. Villian was clearly the better fighter.

As they neared the cave entrance it was clear that there was no-one around, but they still moved cautiously into the open area before the entrance. Villian stared into the strange sky above, judging by the colour it must be nearly noon. During those many nights when they were training, Thanan had told him about the colours on Luminosa, how the sky changed every few hours. The skies on Arcus often changed with the mood of the weather, with the sunrise and the sunsets but nothing like Villian saw here. The sky was an emerald green, seen only in rainbows which showed themselves shyly for a few moments before disappearing, as if they were playing hide and seek.

Villian pulled his eyes away from the sight as Thanan pointed at the cave entrance. He moved forward, his senses on high alert, but the place felt deserted.

They moved to the cave entrance and cautiously made their way inside. The darkness of the cave soon enveloped them. The light from the lantern sap trees which normally lined the route had been removed. It felt different, sinister to Thanan, as they took out their own lights. Maybe it was a trap, but he couldn't feel another presence.

They walked for a while, careful on the slippery floor as the sound of rushing water filled their ears, making it more difficult to hear their enemies. Villian cried out as he lost his footing and nearly fell, but for a steady hand from Thanan. Villian smiled and nodded as he let go of his hand. They waited to see if his scream had given them away, but thankfully they could only hear the water and the thumping of their own hearts. Finally, they came to the entrance to the tunnel and the boat was tied to a post. Thanan opened his mind and spoke to, Pol.

"Are you there?"

"Yes." Came the small voice and Thanan felt relieved that Pol had made it to the other side. He'd worried they would have met a dead end through the network of caves, but Pol was safe and sound and in a short time he would be with his friend and mentor, Tobias. He longed to see his friend and speak to him again. Tell him about his adventures so far and talk about the future and about how he had ridden a dragon.

"Right, Pol is there and everything is okay," Thanan said to Villian.

"*Pol, can you pull the boat a little way and when we come back, I will let you know? If it's anyone other than us, then try and pull the boat all the way to you or run back to the safety of the oasis and we will find you there. We are going to get the children, and then Star and Dragon.*"

It was weird because he could almost feel Pol nodding. That was new. As if Pol didn't need to talk, he just knew they were saying yes. He felt the boat being pulled, and they watched it as it disappeared into the mouth of the tunnel. It was soon out of sight.

"Right. Let's go," Villian said, keen to get moving. They might not have much time once Pathanclaw and Pathandon made themselves known.

They set off into the night as the sky turned dark red, like the darkest sunset Villian had ever seen. It would only be midday to early afternoon on Arcus. Something about the colours in this world made him think about the colours of the dragons. He made a mental note to ask Pathanclaw about all the dragons. He was sure the colours of Luminosa matched the colours of the dragon family, as well as the tattoo which had adorned his arm. It couldn't be a coincidence.

They moved through the forest, alert and slightly afraid. Thanan tried again to communicate with Star but there was still no answer. He wondered where all the other children were. Would they come to their aid when he asked? Would they believe he was here to rescue them? Or did the Masters control extend too far? Could he convince them there was a better life? Although how could he convince them of a better world when he'd not found it. Not seen it. But Villian knew Arcus could be the safe place. They were reaching the outskirts of the camp as Thanan motioned Villian to stop and wait. They peered into the camp but like the cave, everything was still. It was as if they had all disappeared.

They moved silently along the edge of the camp.

Villian was fascinated at this place where Star, Thanan and Pol had lived. It was so basic, like something the shepherds slept in as they moved across the plains back on Arcus, never settling, just a temporary place to lay their head. He saw the food bushes they had spoken off and couldn't resist pulling off a fruit that looked just like an apple. He bit into it and the flavour made his stomach gurgle. It was a mixture of all his favourite foods. It was the best food he had ever tasted. But there was something else, something that should not be. He couldn't work out what it was. Maybe because it was made by magic. He threw it on the floor.

He saw Thanan smiling at him and blushed slightly, knowing he should be concentrating on their mission, but Thanan reached over and picked one for himself, revelling in the pure pleasure. He'd never taken to the trapping of small animals Villian had tried to teach them. He put another one in his pocket, not quite ready to reject this gift of food as Villian was.

There was nothing for them here, so they moved back into the woods and Thanan led them in the direction of where he thought they would be holding Star. They would find the children later. They would need Star and Dragon so they couldn't waste time. The children might still be with the Masters and they would have to let Pathanclaw and Pathandon deal with them for now.

Thanan wondered how they were fairing. Had they reached the female dragons? They'd agreed not to communicate by their minds in case the Masters could somehow listen in. Only for emergencies. They were to let them know when they had Star, Dragon and the children safe before the dragons rescued their kin.

A noise in the woods made them freeze.

It happened so quickly, Star didn't at first have time to register this twist of fate. Triana's hands were glowing as the fire ball formed. Star couldn't believe this would be her end. She looked at Dragon and a feeling of peace came over her, a quietness as she looked into those eyes. She heard Triana finish the spell and felt the heat of the flame as it licked at her skin. This was it, she was going to die right now, on Luminosa, and never escape. This was to be her tomb after all the great deeds she thought she would do. She wouldn't see Thanan or Pol again. Thanan would blame himself, she knew he would. Stupid boy. She would miss fighting with him. Miss growing up together. Miss all the adventures they would have had. Flying on Dragon amongst all the other dragons. Returning to Arcus with Villian and saving his world.

Maybe they would have all settled down and somehow, she would have found her family. Found out where she had come from and see her parents again. In her dreams she often saw two other girls, maybe her sisters? Maybe not. She got the feeling she was the youngest, but it was only ever a fleeting glimpse into a past she didn't know. What could become of Dragon? Would she live if Star died? Star didn't know when she had shut her eyes. But she opened them, knowing she needed to look at Dragon one last time, to let her know it was okay. Thanan would look after Dragon when she was dead. He would come and make sure Dragon survived. He would. She realised she felt no pain. How could there be no pain? Was she already dead? Her eyes searched for Dragon. The sound of screaming filled her mind as she fell to the floor.

Thanan and Villian were clearly on edge, the noise must have just been a branch falling. They carried on their journey through the woods, Thanan couldn't help but reflect on the past. How things had changed. He needed to distract himself from what they would find. Thinking back to the days on the other planet in another time, he remembered it had been a hard day of training and Villian had pushed them further than he thought possible. Every muscle ached. Even his bones hurt, his teeth hurt, and he'd lain grateful in front of the fire as Pathanclaw and Pathandon took up the storytelling each evening.

"What's it like on Suntra, Pathandon? What do dragons do all day?" Star asked. She took a big bite of food and let it dribble down her chin as she was accustomed to do. Prince Villian laughed at her, as Thanan pulled a face. He noticed Star had taken to sitting nearer to Villian when they settled for the night. He felt a stab of jealousy run through him. It confused him as he and Star were friends and Prince Villian was engaged so it shouldn't matter. He brushed his thoughts to one side as he listened to Pathandon. He hoped the other dragons weren't listening and blushed.

"We start the day with stories, telling of the past and present and thoughts of the future. Unlike humans we cannot write our history down. It has to be passed through stories or it will be forgotten."

"We used to do that," Thanan said.

"What do you mean, Thanan. Do you remember something before Luminosa?" Star had stopped eating now and was staring at him intently.

Thanan looked shocked, as if he hadn't meant to speak. "I don't know. I'm not sure where that came from. I don't really remember doing that."

"Sometimes when we are relaxed and let our minds find the memories, it can unlock thoughts you didn't know were hidden," Pathanclaw said. *"Don't force it, Thanan. Don't try and search for them, just let them come."*

Thanan nodded. He tried to settle his mind instead of following this thin thread of memory which dangled out of the darkness of his mind. Over the last moons of storytelling Thanan had felt something being released in him. His dreams were vivid, and he woke to wisps of images. He and Star had spoken to Pathanclaw about it. He'd suggested that whatever power was on Luminosa it might block their memories as well as their magic.

He'd asked Triana if the same was happening to her but she said no, despite him witnessing the look in her eyes when she woke up: before she'd guarded her reactions. Thanan had spoken to Villian many times about the children and Villian often marvelled that they were so grown up at such a young age. Although during breaks in training on Arcus, Dyana had told him about how the children were treated where she came from. It was something he would address when he became king. He knew he hadn't had the same childhood as most, but he accepted it was his role in life to make sure the kingdom was a good place to live. He didn't intend to make the same mistakes as his father and the kings before him.

"Suntra is a beautiful giving planet. It is rich in life and as I've told you before, dragons only take what they need. We are protectors and not takers but like every living thing, we need to eat. This is the natural order."

"Maybe magic dragons are going to be the new order," Triana said. She rarely spoke to them during their story telling.

"I have thought about this. Seeing Star with Dragon, I cannot see how it seems wrong that two species have come together but they have not been created naturally. It has been forced on you."

"But magic comes from dragons, from you. So how can you say that is not natural?" Thanan asked. He hoped it wasn't rude to speak to a dragon this way, but Pathanclaw didn't seem to mind.

"I understand what you're saying, but humans should have never been given the power. They are too used to

taking advantage of situations and using things for their own gain instead of for others."

"Well, maybe it wasn't an accident that they learnt magic. Maybe that was as it should be. I like using magic. It seems wrong not to have magic in my body, like some part of me is missing," Thanan said.

"I don't know all the answers, Thanan. It is something we will need to discover together once this is over. One thing I do know is that the Masters cannot be allowed to continue as they are. Right or wrong, what they are doing should not be allowed. If humans are to learn magic, if that is their fate, they should not be made to do it and be taken from their families. It must be a choice. It cannot continue to happen. Let us not forget the Masters have also stolen our female dragons."

Thanan felt the sorrow from the two dragons. As much as he didn't want to return to Luminosa, he feared the dragons wouldn't be able to save their kin and they would pay the price. They had passed the age of leaving, so even though they had a comfortable life in the camp, for the most part, it wouldn't be their fate if they made it back.

"Suntra, is very much like the lands we're on now. After morning stories, the younglings would go to train, whilst the elders sorted out any matters that need our attention. We often discussed what the future might hold, what we would do when we found the females dragons and returned to our home of Arcus. If indeed we should return. Who would stay behind?"

"What do you mean, stay behind? Why would anyone stay behind?"

Pathanclaw knew this answer would provoke a response in Pathandon. He was not aware of the Elders' discussions.

"You know our power comes from the gems. We channel the power through the guardians. It has always been our intention to close the portals once we returned to Arcus. To

do this requires great power and so, some will have to stay behind. A guardian at the very least. But some of the elders may also need to stay behind to ensure their protection. If the enemy turned up to stop them, we would need some to be able protect the guardians for the precious time we would need to close the portals forever."

"But why not keep them open? Why close them at all?"

"Because we have already seen the damage which has been done through creating these portals. They were created in desperation to escape and to that end, they protected our species. But once we are back on Arcus, we will not run again. We will fight our foes and if we are defeated then we will accept that is our fate. We have created too much imbalance and threat to other worlds. We believed our survival was above the effect on others and we were wrong."

The children didn't quite understand everything, but they felt Pathanclaw's emotion. Now Thanan knew that if they were to lay the blame at anyone, it would be him. His friendship with Raykan had caused much pain and suffering but without it, Star wouldn't have had Dragon and Thanan and she wouldn't be best friends. It hurt Thanan's brain when he thought about what could have been if they hadn't been taken to serve the Masters on Luminosa. It sounded like no other planet held the changing colours as Luminosa did.

"Maybe this was all supposed to happen. Perhaps you were supposed to teach magic to Raykan and all of this should have happened," Thanan said.

Pathanclaw liked this simple view. He clung to the hope it was true because maybe he didn't need to keep blaming himself for his folly all those years ago. He hoped this young child with a pure heart was right.

Thanan put his hand up to stop Villian as they made it to the clearing. The underground prison was just ahead. He hoped Star and Dragon were still alive.

Chapter 17 – Suntra

General Bluewing was proud of how the younglings were progressing, they had followed his leadership. They all knew the seriousness of the situation and soon they would be called upon by their king to fight and regain the world most of them had never lived on. There was excitement in the air. If the females were found, then the younglings would have mates and hopefully new females would be born to continue their legacy. Without them, they would diminish. Not for thousands of years, but one day they would fly no longer.

It was the day Queen Silvarna was to return to the cave and partake in an act which might mean the end of her long life, a blessed life for the majority. She had known peace from a young age and throughout much of her life and for this she was truly grateful. For her part now she only hoped they could warn her beloved and save the future, save the females and return home. The thought of hearing his voice one more time, even if it was across another time, another planet. She would give anything for his voice, she would give her life. She put the discussion with Kyanite to the back of her mind.

They had not told the other dragons of the danger to her, but they needn't be worried. The council felt it better to let the others focus on what they needed to do. General Bluewing would escort her once again, as was right and the rest would hope to see them both flying back to the safety of the group, their mission accomplished. Queen Silvarna was to try and find out when Pathanclaw could be expected to return. Luckily, dragons didn't have 'things' as did humans. The times she had flown over a hamlet, town, a city and seen all the things these humans needed to live, to survive, the clothes they needed to protect them, it was a wonder how they ever survived. A dragon needed nothing but fire in their belly, a wide-open sky and each other. She had often thought their lack of material wealth was the reason they thrived, but then they had been born with everything they needed to survive.

On this beautiful fine day she decided to join in the training, as so long ago when she and Pathanclaw had complained at their aching bodies, she would once again feel the delight of the younglings and maybe teach them a thing or two. If this were to be her last day, then she would have fun and pass on the memories which the younglings would take into old age.

While General Bluewing was settling them down, Silvarna felt lightness in her heart once again. Bluewing and Pathandon were always dedicated to their training but they were often the ones who tried to get away to do their own thing. The competition fierce between them. It was interesting to see how the dynamics had changed with the younglings. Their number on Suntra now totalled forty-four, including the two now fighting for their freedom. The younglings seemed to need time to adapt to this change in their midst and Silvarna was proud they were all trying so hard.

She watched them as they lined up in their battle formation. There was always competition between the Silver hunters; the Gold dragons, who were ferocious fighters and the Blues who always thought their place was at the front because they needed to protect the royal dragons. Today they'd decided to have Queen Silvarna in position and under attack. It had been something Battlewing had insisted they practice, despite dragons never having to fight dragons before on Suntra. It worried Silvarna about what they would face when they eventually returned to Arcus. She had complete faith they would all return, she just hoped it would be the homecoming they wanted.

General Bluewing had finished ordering his troops, "*We are ready, Queen Silvarna.*" He'd split the younglings so brother faced brother. The tension was palpable. There was honour at stake.

Silvarna obligingly flew into the air above them, with a sad thought of when she and Pathanclaw had shared training sessions with the dragons. She cleared her mind and focused on the fight.

Blueblaze and Blueclaw moved into position, one on each side of their Queen as the Blue should be. They would repeat this many times with each dragon taking a different place so they could all protect the Queen no matter what happened.

Longsong flew into position behind Queen Silvarna. Bluewing had been instrumental in coaxing the Greens out. They were able to channel the most powerful magic from the gems. Normally they would be in the cave, but Bluewing felt it was important for the other dragons to know who was helping them. They were much smaller than the other dragons, their skills did not lay in hunting or fighting. The Greens normally spent many hours still and in thought, mastering and harnessing the power of magic. They rarely joined in with the others, but even they seemed excited by this spectacle.

Two silvers, Goch and Saydn, moved in front of the queen as by two Nuri and Kynarax covered the rear. The circle around the queen was formed. Firelight flew below to watch for an attack. If they could work together, they would be a force. The formation would work even better when they all fought together.

The attacking force gathered. Daysong their Green

dragon did not join the fight, but at a safe distance, was channelling when needed. Hellevore whose two sisters were lost was not happy about being left out, but Bluewing was prepared for a change he would need to make. Bluebeard, Bluelightening, Agnax, Shadv, Shimmer, Venathrax and Enoir waited for the signal. Shadv always felt his sister Sneddon was with him when he fought.

General Bluewing had been testing the protection team with different formation and dragons to try and find the strongest team. This time it was stacked for Queen Silvarna's team if they held formation. Ember had allowed his son Ritikus to join them. A great privilege. Ritikus wouldn't fight, but he was a mastermind in tactics.

Queen Silvarna marvelled at how quickly the dragons had learned to fight as one. Dragons had fought many thousands of years in the past, but for generations before Silvarna was born they had been at peace. However, the paths of the dragon families had been set. The memory of dragons and their history had triggered this skill. It was a shame so many had been killed on Arcus before they'd had realised their peril and left.

They were flying as one now, following General Bluewing's orders. Blueblaze and Blueclaw from each side dropped below so they were shadowing Silvarna, protecting her from an attack from the ground with Firelight moving above, in case they were attacked by humans. Still, many of them thought this would never happen again. Humans were so insignificant compared to dragons but General Battlewing had insisted from the day they arrived on Suntra they would protect the Reds from all sides, would protect them against any threat, human or otherwise.

As the Blues dropped, Ritikus prepared to create the protection spell. This would form a bubble around the group protecting them from all threats. It would give them a precious few moments to locate where they were being attacked from.

A flame shot past Blueclaw and he dropped down and out of the bubble which was forming. Blueclaw was the most jittery of the dragons and any slight sound would have him curled up on the floor. The others tried to support him, but fighting just wasn't his role, despite being a Blue. General Bluewing needed to know their weaknesses. Blueclaw was a good spotter.

"You're out, Blueclaw. Return to the ground. Hellevore take his place."

The Elders were monitoring the battle and judged when a fatal blow would render them out of the real battle. They were, of course, not to use all their skills or flames, but enough for a little singe would mean 'The End' in real battle.

"Nuri, Hellevore what are you doing?" Bluewing demanded. "Where are we being attacked from? Ritikus get that shield up now. Your Queen is under attack."

"Shadv, Bluebeard, Enori and Venathrax must have been made invisible to Daysong. I can just see their outline above. Engaging now."

Shadv and Vynarax swooped to the side as the others closed rank.

"Where are the others?"

"Cannot see them yet, I think they are holding back," Goch replied, his eyes scanning the horizon.

"Nuri, Vynarax, make sure you cover Ember. We cannot afford to lose the shield."

"I've found them," Goch declared, unable to hide the excitement from his thoughts.

"Right, do not attack. It could be a trick to lure us out. They have already lessened our number, let's not make it so easy next time. Stick to the plan," Bluewing ordered.

The pack reached the mountains. As they made their way over the top the large bulls that grazed so far in the mountains scattered and the noise of great stampede reverberated throughout the air.

"Now," General Bluewing ordered.

They peeled off and took up the rear, just as the other group arrived into view. It was as Bluewing thought, they could only use magic for so long to keep the dragons invisible. It was the one weakness of a dragon. They needed to recharge to use their magic.

As the attackers flew faster at the sight of their brothers heading for them knowing they had advantage over the four heading their way, the black guardian realised the plan slightly too late. He tried to warn the group but they had fixed their minds on destroying the pack and winning the day. As Bluewing hoped, they had miscalculated that they had the winning plan. Too confident and not thinking ahead. Saydn and Blueblaze went high and Hellevore dropped below as they avoided a full collision in the air. Wings touching wings and flames missing their targets, the attackers turned to finish their prey.

"Watch out," Ritikus roared. Shadv and Enori turned to see the other half of the circle had split from the pack and were not protecting the Queen. This was their chance.

"Attack the Queen's shielding now, we have them. They've all split up," roared Bluelightening in their minds

Longsong flew ahead, not waiting for the protection of the others. Being used to a solitary life this was overwhelming and she longed for the gem cave. This had been a bad idea.

"No!" roared, Ritikus again. "You are leaving us vulnerable."

General Bluewing was surprised how well Ritikus had taken to warfare. But his warning was ignored. Bluebeard and Bluelightening went into a death roll heading for Longsong. Firelight looked up and forged a shielding spell just in time as the dragons' mouths opened and he was engulfed in flames. He swore he could hear his brothers laughing. As the Blues passed, he saw the Golds and Silvers in a ferocious battle, but they were outnumbered and Nuri had managed to break away. He realised the Queen was vulnerable as was Longsong. Queen Silvarna was desperate to get into the battle, but General Bluewing had insisted she play her part.

"With me, now, before they return to the Queen and Longsong." Daysong started forming the spell to break their hold on the queen as they forged ahead. They could see the pack far ahead flying over one of the large pools which disappeared into the distance.

"We have them. Just keep moving. They only have two left to defeat. The others are on our tail and after the blues." Nuri declared.

Daysong had no space to think, her focus on breaking the spell the only room in her mind. Her target was dead ahead. The blues came in to attack again but she glided and moved avoiding their attack. It was as if they were one. So close to the pack now. Goch could see his brother Agnax. They could do this.

It worked. The protection shield fell apart and Daysong's team roared in delight. They were going to win. The others were on their way. The rest of the dragons broke away and turned to face them. General Bluewing watched from the air as he saw the gap to the Queen widening. What were they doing? Too late, the black dragon cried to them yet again. "It's a trap, get out of there." It was too late.

The Elders called Daysong's team the winners and they all landed on the training ground, all except Longsong who had had enough and returned to the gem cave. Fighting was not her role as a dragon.

"Well done, Daysong's team. But remember we can only use that tactic once. An intelligent army would not normally be drawn out so easily to break formation and leave the one they were supposed to be protecting!"

There was mirth amongst the winners. Longsong's team felt a bit embarrassed. General Bluewing knew the greatest danger they faced was not only their inexperience but a dragons natural way was to attack in battle and not sit back waiting for the enemy to come to them. It was a part of them.

Despite their loss, they all left satisfied. General Bluewing had made them re-enact the battle in their minds, seeing the weakness in each other. The silver dragons left to hunt for the evening food and the blues gathered to talk strategy. They teased Bluebeard good naturedly about being the first one to get taken out. He didn't mind really, he hated battles anyway.

Chapter 18 – Arcus

Lady Cartina's mouth dropped at the sight of her sister. How could she be here? One of the agreements she had made with her parents was that her sister wasn't allowed to come to the kingdom. Lady Cartina glared at her father, who had the decency to look abashed. It was a betrayal of trust and he knew it. But there was more to his look. Maybe he hadn't known.

Lady Cartina smiled sweetly and moved to her sister's side, "Why sister, what a surprise. How lovely to see you here."

Her sister turned her haughty, entitled gaze and looked her up and down. Even now, betrothed to a Prince and on course to become the Queen of Arcus, she still quivered under her sister's judgement, and judgement there was.

From children they had disliked each other. Their personalities were so different. Servants would scurry from her sister, whereas with her they would pass the time of day and enjoy a kind word. Lady Cartina had often helped the servants, taking their difficulties to her father but packaging the requests in a way he couldn't refuse. He knew what she was doing but as long as she asked in the right way, he was happy to indulge her. If his daughters were happy, it would save the accusations from their mother.

Helendy was like their father but far more ruthless and desperate for power. She knew the servants would make the sign to ward away evil when she passed. In contrast to

Lady Cartina, her sister had dark features, long braided hair swept up and pulled back, which gave her a constant look of distain. Helendy's sun-darkened skin reflected her love of hunting and not a day went by when she didn't ride the horses. So different to her complexion, her love of books and things that were supposed to be wifely attributes kept her indoors. Her sister born only a year later than her but her freedom caused a bitterness that would mean they would never be close. Her sister coveted power and Helendy had been furious when her parents and the party left for the kingdom without her. Helendy did not wave them off but Lady Cartina had felt her sister's eyes stick daggers into her back as she rode towards her sister's one desire.

"It is wonderful to see you again, sister. May I congratulate you on your upcoming marriage. I hope the prince returns soon." Helendy bowed just short of custom. Her words were said with an edge no other would be able to detect, except maybe her mother, who moved closer, in case her daughters forgot themselves. They were in the presence of the king and rumours had been flying around the court that Prince Villian had disappeared conveniently after the marriage had been announced. There were some who suspected or gossiped foul play. The courtiers were always ready to fill their boring lives with intrigue, rarely caring that their lies might mean the death for another. It was all part of the game.

"Thank you, my sister. I am very happy but also beside myself with worry. I pray every day for Prince Villian to return to me and we can be wed in this great hall and welcome my new parents, the King and Queen of Arcus."

She felt the rage from her sister. She knew those words would cut her deep and yet she couldn't help herself. Her sister brought out the worst in her despite her attempts to stop these negative feelings. What was it that her own blood could cause so much hurt and upset. Should they not be the best of friends, happy for each other? But it wouldn't be their path. She had tried many times.

"It is wonderful to have my family back in one place," Lady Cartina's father addressed the king. "I thank your majesty for the wonderful surprise. Our daughters will have many days' news to catch up on."

The king didn't look at all interested in the proceedings, but Lady Cartina caught his glance as he looked over Helendy. Cartina noted that her sister had opted for a very low-cut dress, which the Queen had clearly already noticed when her gaze swept over her sister. Lady Cartina felt a shiver run throughout her body. She couldn't let her sister spoil this for her. When Prince Villian returned from his quest, they would be married. He would be hailed the hero of Arcus and his place surely would soon be on the throne. The rumours of the king's ill health were another rumour amongst the courtiers but this one was borne out by the king's pallor and cough that never seemed to give him a moment's peace.

Soon the court was cleared and Lady Cartina was left wondering why she had been summoned. Was it to show her parents that if Prince Villian didn't return he had the whole family here to be held accountable? But what did that matter? The King could get to her sister if he so desired. Would the protectors of their homelands really wage a war against the kingdom if anything happened to their family? She hoped so, their people were loyal. But as she left the room, she caught the sly smile of Baynard and shuddered. There were men like him everywhere.

Her maid, Luciana, said that Ironhand and the Keeper of Books had been shocked to hear Baynard was still alive. They said Prince Villian had dealt a killer blow and he'd looked like his evil soul had been separate from his body. But he was alive and well. The Keeper had not looked happy, Luciana recounted. How had he healed his body so fast?

As the large doors closed behind them, Lady Cartina turned to her sister.

"What are you really doing here?" she hissed.

"Not here," her father commanded, "meet me in my chambers. Now."

He strode off without waiting for them.

"Are you not pleased to see me, dear sister? It's a shame you've lost your Prince so quickly. How careless of you."

Lady Cartina bit her tongue. She should never had engaged with her sister. It was a mistake. If she ignored her then it usually had the same effect, as Helendy hated to be ignored.

"Shh, until we are in your father's chambers." Her mother came between them and guided them in silence to the relative safety of their rooms in a separate wing of the castle.

Once the door had been closed her father spoke, "Why are you here, Helendy?"

Her sister looked momentarily shocked, which was unusual for her. "Because you asked me to come? A servant from the castle came and said that you needed me here."

Their father picked up a goblet and took a long drink before wiping his mouth, "This is disturbing news. I did not send for you. Having all the family together makes us weak. While one of our kin is at the castle, we had strength. I was thinking of sending your mother back to be with you. But the time has passed."

Their mother paled and perched on the nearest chair. Her sister was unnaturally quiet. Maybe she'd realised the place which she had left was perhaps the safest place for her. Now she had entered the real game, not the pretend one where she was the one in control. In this moment, her sister might have just grown up, but Lady Cartina doubted it would make her play a less dangerous game.

"What should we do?" her mother asked.

"At the moment, nothing. If the Prince returns unharmed then there is nothing to worry about. If not, then I have people ready to get you away safely."

"I cannot believe you have lost your Prince," Helendy said scornfully.

"Hush your childish words. We are in great danger here. Words like that will have our family strung up on the battlements. Don't you realise the danger?"

Helendy flushed at her father's rebuke. Even though they had similar personalities, their father rarely had a bad word said against his younger daughter, the one they all knew he wished had been born first. She had his drive and need for power. She and her mother shared the opposite. The presence of them both in the same room could be stifling.

"Sorry, father. I didn't mean to cause offence. Please forgive me."

Her father moved to her and squeezed her arm gently to show he felt no ill will.

"Maybe we should leave now if we are in that much danger. Maybe it's not wise to stay," her mother said anxiously.

Lady Cartina felt her stomach turn. She couldn't leave with her family now. She had to be ready to meet the others and escape. She felt bad about leaving her mother and father but if she left then she doubted the King would harm them. She had contrived to make it look like she had been kidnapped. Luciana was a most convincing actress when called upon. She was to say that Lady Cartina had been kidnapped from the grounds when she was on her evening walk and make it look like it was the enemy. That way it would absolve the rumours away from their family. If she had been taken, then they couldn't have anything to do with Prince Villian's kidnapping.

Lady Cartina twisted the ring slowly. Where was he now? When would he be back? The Keeper thought it could be months before he returned, but what about the imminent threat here? Would he make it back in time to save them? So much relied on him returning. Was it a girl's hope that everything would be well? Was she so naïve about what was to come? The possibility of losing Prince Villian without truly getting to know him was too much. She felt slightly faint and reached her hand out to brace herself. Closing her eyes, she breathed deeply taking control. She needed to be stronger. Look how much she had already done. Bringing Ironhand, the Keeper, the warriors and hopefully Raykan together. She had helped to make that possible.

When she opened her eyes, her sister was appraising her with an odd look. Maybe she was noticing her sister had grown up since she last saw her, but that would only make her seem more like competition to her. Her sister's gaze returned to her father.

"No, we will stay here. It wouldn't look good if we left as if we had something to hide. While we are here, the king will feel that he has the upper hand. We continue as normal but I will have extra guards posted."

"Surely that will make us look as if we have something to hide. Would it not be better to carry on as you have said but just take more care?" Lady Cartina spoke and noticed with satisfaction that she had beaten her sister as she watched her mouth close into a snarl.

A look of respect passed her father's face, once again, which she was not used to.

"You're right, of course. But limit where you go. Do not leave your chambers unless it is for engagements you are required to do. No more walks in the evening and I will post extra guards."

Lady Cartina was about to protest, but kept quiet. She needed free movement, but by drawing attention to it would make it harder. It would be harder to leave than she first thought.

Children – Luminosa

As they came through the clearing, Galan saw Kyla chained and gagged. He felt relief at first. She was alive, that was all he could think about for now. The children moved forward, trying not to gasp at the size of the dragons also chained. A whisper went through them: 'Suckers.' These were the things that were blocking their magic. What Triana had told them when she returned was true after all. One of the dragons moved slightly and the chains sounded too loud making one of the boys scream. Galan touched his shoulder and quietened him down. He felt the Masters would have no patience today.

A glint to his right made him turn to look up into the giant mountains which ran along a ridge, far past this sandy death valley as he could now see it. The red of the day was making the ground glimmer with blood crystals. The hairs on his arm tingled. What was to become of them? He realised it wasn't just the scene before him. The block had been taken off. The children looked at each wide eyed. The Masters had allowed them access to their magic. But it was not only that, it felt stronger somehow.

Moments later the children, who had them, were joined by their creatures. The children talked about their creatures and sometimes had their free time in camp, but they were never all together like this. Galan marvelled at the sight of them. The majority had dragons, a few of the younger ones had small lizards. It suddenly struck him that it was the strong older children who had the dragons as creatures. Not one child past the age of ten didn't have a dragon. Galan had named his dragon, Pomal, thinking the name sounded familiar. Galan moved to its side and placed his hand on the scaled head. Only waist height, it didn't have the feathers as Star's dragon had. Pomal looked more like the dragons behind him.

He looked into the distance again. Something, there was something but it was too far to see. Instinct made him seek out Kyla. Her eyes were defiant. Galan frowned at the sudden change in her eyes which had widened. He saw confusion, fear and then a massive grin stretched out from behind the gag. What was going on? Was this what Star had meant by being ready? Were they to finally defy the Masters and take back control? Had the others really come back to rescue them?

Chapter 19 – Luminosa

It was too late, Triana formed one fireball after another. Her mind filled with anger, pain and disappointment at how the Masters had treated her when she returned. She had done so much for them. It was leader who had given her the talisman and told her what to do when the time came. He knew all along they would return for the other dragons and he welcomed their return. They needed more gems. It was becoming difficult to harness the power they needed. There were more problems she knew they didn't care to share with her. She was only important to do what they needed and then she was cast aside like she was nothing.

When they'd locked Star and her Dragon away, Triana had met with the Master, the one who had favoured her from the beginning, giving her more than the other children when she informed on them. She'd helped them to choose the right children. She had a talent for knowing which would be able to harness the magic and which were useless. It was funny how some of the children were just that. They had no special talents. It was as if they were immune to magic, as if they didn't have the capacity within them.

She'd thought that the Masters would let her go home now. They had promised her many things if she helped them and spied on Thanan, Star and Pol. They would make her a Master and then even send her home, even though she didn't know where home was. She'd bragged to all the other children that she remembered her parents and convinced them they had wanted her to come to this place so she could learn magic. The new children were always in awe of her tales of home, but sadly, that's all they were. Tales. Over the years she'd spoken to the new children and many of them had been able to hold on to a few thin threads of another life. She had used this information and eventually she didn't really know what the truth was anymore; where her memories ended, and the stolen ones interwove. She had built a whole past for herself which she knew deep down wasn't real.

In the long nights when she'd laid in her hammock, she'd closed her eyes tight and clenched her fists, trying to remember her parents, but she couldn't trust her memories anymore. She didn't know if these kind people looking at her were her mother and father, or her imagination. The Master had told her that her parents waited for her return. But even now the Masters' said they needed more from her. She had shouted then when he'd said they wouldn't return her yet and had paid for her disobedience. At that point she had wondered if she had made a terrible mistake in trusting the Masters. Had they been using her all along to find out about that freak, Pol and to make sure the dragons returned? How had the Masters known where they would end up and that the dragons would be there? If only she had such knowledge, such power and could make others do what she wanted.

She had done their bidding when she returned and told the children a story about the dragons, how they had once come to this land and tried to kill everyone. This was how the Suckers came to be. Triana enjoyed the power she had over the young children, they were transfixed and their mouths hung open when they learned the Suckers were dragons. It frustrated her that the Masters wouldn't tell her why they used the dragons to steal magic and what they were doing with it. The gems were important for the magic but she didn't know how it all fitted together.

Triana held the children in rapture as she told them she'd been sent on mission to bring back Thanan, Star and Pol when they had fled to bring back the mighty dragons to kill them all, telling them that dragons ate children. The children were so stupid, they didn't question that Thanan and Star were children and were riding the dragons. The children were so naive. She was nearly eleven now and knew more than anyone in camp. Galan had eyed her with distrust, but mostly they believed her but in her heart, she knew the dragons weren't bad. Pathanclaw and Pathandon had been nothing but nice to her even though they knew she was hiding something. Maybe the dragons would have helped her get home. But it was all too late now.

After she'd finished telling her story, she'd led the children through the forest. Triana had been shocked to hear that Star had been right about the Suckers. Another thing that the Master's had not told her. As the children followed her, the thoughts brewed in her mind. She became angrier and angrier, thinking about how Star had mocked her and always tried to belittle her. Her footsteps matched her mood and suddenly she whirled around.

"You," Triana pointed at Galan, "lead them all straight down there until you reach the end of the forest. The Masters will be waiting for you. I have other things to do."

Triana stalked off not waiting for an answer, confident they would do as they were told, her anger bubbling like a volcano. It was all Star's fault. She would make her pay for everything. Maybe then the Masters would send her home. They would realise she could be ruthless like them, and that she deserved to be treated as an equal. She would have great power like them. She could feel the magic thrumming through her hypersensitive body. It made everything tingle. She could feel all the tiny hairs on a leaf as it caressed her face as she ran faster and faster through the woods. She had power and she would use it. All her anger was focused on Star, the only one who had defied her. It had made her look weak to the Masters. That's why they didn't give her what she wanted. Because of Star. Her and her stupid dragon. Triana would not make that mistake again.

The screaming made her return to the present. She looked at her glowing hands wondering what she had done before falling to the ground.

Star didn't know when she stopped screaming. She wondered how she could still scream when she was dead. She heard other noises. Voices. She thought maybe it was Thanan and Villian come to rescue her but she couldn't really make out the words.

Star couldn't move, couldn't lift her head, couldn't open her eyes. Nothing would work. Moments later she felt hands lift her slightly and Thanan's face filled her vision as he pulled up her eyelid. She would have smacked him if she'd been alive.

"Star, it's me? Thanan. Do you know who I am?"

She might have laughed at him. Of course she knew who he was. But now, maybe she didn't know. Now that she was dead. Did that mean Thanan was dead as well? Had Triana killed them all? It made her sad and glad. Sad that Thanan had died, but glad he was with her. It would make death easier. They might have fun being dead together.

"I think she's in shock, Villian. We need to get her out of here, and fast. She's too big to carry on my own. You need to help me."

"Let me just finish tying Triana up."

"Why don't you kill her? Look what she has done. She doesn't deserve to be alive." Thanan's voice broke and Star wanted to do something. She tried to move her arms but they wouldn't work. It was as if everything was disconnected. She supposed if you were dead that's how it would be. A wave of overwhelming sadness hit her, she was dead and so were Thanan and Villian it seemed. He wouldn't be able to take the dragons and fulfil his quest to save Arcus. He wouldn't marry Lady Cartina, although she was sort of pleased about that. It would mean that Pol would be alone. Alone in this world without their friends. Pol would have no-one to talk to or protect her. A sob escaped her lips. She didn't think death would be so emotional.

"Star, Star. Don't cry. Please don't cry. We will get you away from here. Don't worry."

Star felt Thanan adjust his position and his arms settled under her armpits and she presumed it was Villian who was gripping her legs. She didn't think she would be able to feel so much when she was dead. They moved slowly in the tight space. She was starting to think maybe she was alive. But why wasn't she burnt to a crisp, she'd felt the heat from the fireball? How could she be alive? Thanan sounded worried but not as if she'd had her face burnt off. She thought back to a time when she had been training Dragon. They had laid on the grass as she wanted to teach Dragon how to control her flame, and Thanan had been worried about Dragon burning her face off, but she'd said she would look like the cool scarred dragon lady and didn't mind. She still wouldn't mind.

As they moved out of the cell, Star was starting to believe she was really alive, but something didn't feel right. There was an emptiness that hadn't been there before. Like a hole somewhere deep inside her. Her senses were coming back and she could hear things, feel things. She managed to focus on the shape on the floor. Triana was tied up and unconscious. She had a long bleeding gash on her forehead. She looked dead, but she must still be breathing because she thought she heard Thanan tell

Villian to kill her. Maybe he had, and no matter how hard she tried, she couldn't feel sorry for Triana. She was glad the girl was dead even though she knew Pol would frown at her for thinking it.

"Let's get her outside and then I will be able to carry her. Thanan you can scout ahead. We need to get out of here. Can Pathanclaw help us?"

Thanan was grunting and Star thought, 'I'm not that heavy.' She would have scolded him once but now it didn't seem to matter and she couldn't find her voice. She was too tired to do anything. If she really wasn't dead and had been rescued by her friends, she wanted to go to sleep. She hoped they were getting Dragon. She relaxed knowing Thanan wouldn't leave her behind.

"Pathanclaw says they cannot help. The Masters are there with the children. He says we need to get away and they will keep them distracted. He said some children are on their way to the cave. We need to get back and get them to safety."

A scream that felt like it would tear their hearts out echoed around the cell walls.

Pathanclaw was worried about Thanan, Villian and Star. He didn't like leaving them alone to fend for themselves. It wasn't the way. He and Pathandon should be with them. But they needed to rescue the female dragons and if they went in quietly, he hoped Thanan and Villian would be able to get the others to safety.

As the sky had turned from red to purple, Pathanclaw wondered at the similarities to the dragon family. This could be no coincidence that the colours on Luminosa matched the colours of the dragon families. He'd tried not to be too interested when Thanan and Star had spoken about Luminosa, but he was sure that at least Villian would have picked up on it. The young prince rarely missed anything.

Could Luminosa be the place where dragons had been born and not Arcus. This world felt somehow familiar but not home as Arcus had always been. Was that because he had not been born of this world? Is this why Barakar had come to this world? Because magic was stronger here and he was able to harness this to build his powers and that of the children. Barakar only ever had his own interests at heart. He and his brother were night and day in every way. Pathanclaw wondered what Raykan would think when he heard his brother was alive and that he had not perished all those years ago. Maybe he already knew, had suspected as Pathanclaw did. They both had a part to play in releasing this evil onto the world.

He and Pathandon landed on a mountain top, many miles away from where the female dragons were. His eyes fixed back on them immediately, taking in the Masters and children who had now lined up in front of them. Pathanclaw could see their heads turn only slightly in his direction, the heavy muzzles an insult to their freedom. He swept across the line of dragons, to finally find the females and see the hope that the history of the dragons could go on. It was a sight to behold.

All the families were represented, all except the purple dragons. Would they ever come back? The disappearance after they'd had to leave Arcus had been yet another shock at the time. The purples had always kept their distance; they were the thinkers, they understood the earth, how they fitted into the worlds better than any of the other families. They were in touch with the very essence of power. He knew one was in their midst, hidden, maybe even from themselves. Would they return when it was safe? When they had learned what they needed to know?

Pathanclaw couldn't comprehend the power Barakar had accumulated. He was the very worst of what a human could be. He used this gift of magic for evil, to hurt others and for personal gain. Not to help and make others' lives better, not to sustain the very earth which gave him life. But then he thought about his friend Raykan, who delighted in his gift and had never used it to harm another, even though if he had killed his brother, they might have had to leave the safety of Arcus.

The colours of the dragons were muted due to the sand which covered their bodies. A glint of silver from the scales of Anark and Sneddon caught his attention as a slight movement made Pathanclaw aware that they knew of the presence of their king and were ready. It was a joy to behold as he looked down the line, seeing more than just the chains. They were royal dragons, Manaya and Ruby. His heart rejoiced that their line could continue. It had been his hope Pathandon and Ruby would be the next rulers. Bluesong and Bluelightening flanked either side of the reds, protecting their royal dragons even when they could offer no protection other than comfort at their presence. His heart leapt with hope as he saw sisters, Hellebore, Hayan, their one remaining sister on Suntra mourned their loss, and Nelori, calm and thoughtful Nelori. Finally, his eyes rested on the green scales of Echosong and Greysong. They alone had the ability to harness the power of the gems. They, along with Allanor, the Black dragon who was chained in the middle, were Barakar's greatest gift. What horrors had they endured all these years?

Pathanclaw didn't know why he couldn't speak to them directly. Their minds were closed to his. Barakar was somehow blocking their communication. But how? How was he using the dragons? Thanan and Star told him the Suckers, as they had known them, had stopped them from forming magic when they were in camp, a way to control the children and their creatures.

Humans had not been magic users. Maybe this was a

gift the dragons had. But what was the advantage to Barakar? Surely he didn't need the dragons just for this? It was a big risk to have taken the dragons and Pathanclaw wondered how he achieved this feat. How had he had such power back then? What trick had he used to imprison such mighty dragons as these?

"Grandfather. Look."

Pathandon was aware his grandfather was deep in thought. He was shocked by the sight of the female dragons in chains but he was pleased they would not be the last of the dragons. The younglings all felt the responsibility if they would be the last of the dragons.

As they watched, the sky seemed to shrink, the colours swirling around the dragons, children and Masters. A forcefield had been formed when they'd arrived. Pathanclaw rebuked himself. He should have acted sooner, not given them time to react. After all Barakar knew they were here and he would know they'd come for the dragons.

Barakar's attention was focused in their direction. He couldn't see them, surely, they were too far away.

"My friends, King Pathanclaw." Barakar's voice reached them loud and clear. "It's nice to see you again. What a shame you left so suddenly since we have a lot to catch up on. I've sent one of my Masters with the children to meet with Thanan, Star and the new boy, Prince Villian. I must thank you for bringing me new children. It's not been easy taking them from Arcus just lately. There is great unrest. I must return soon and put matters back in order. But first..."

Chapter 20 – Suntra

It was time to make the journey to the gem cave. Queen Silvarna could not put this dangerous deed off any longer. If today was to be the day she died, then so be it. But now she was also making the choice for another. Kyanite had once again tried to change her mind. But it was set. She would do this. Had to do this. Not only to help everyone but she also knew for selfish reasons she had to hear Pathanclaw's voice one more time.

It was a sombre morning as she left with General Bluewing. Even though only the council knew the perils, the others felt something was wrong. There was a finality in the air, it would be a day of change.

Queen Silvarna tried to reassure the others before she left. She and Bluewing were silent during the long journey to the cave. Everything had been said and they each had their own thoughts to process. As before, Ember met them at the cave entrance and once inside, Longsong joined them.

"I have heard much about your training, General Bluewing. I fear Ritikus may want to join your battles rather than do his duty here," Ember said to Bluewing as they made their way inside.

"We were lucky to have him there. It does us all good to realise who we are fighting for."

"That it does, General."

They entered the large cave and again Queen Silvarna felt despair at the grey scar which ran through the shining gems. She thought it had become bigger, even in the last few days.

"Before we go ahead, there is something else we need to discuss." The seriousness of Ember's words made Bluewing and Silvarna look up. Could there be more? They both waited.

"We have had long discussions since you left and we need to protect the gems. This, above all else, is our priority. We need to close the portal on Suntra as soon as possible."

"What does that mean?" General Bluewing asked, his mind already thinking through the possibilities. Could they leave? When? How was it possible without King Pathanclaw?

"Hush," Queen Silvarna spoke directly to him. But it wasn't an order. General Bluewing closed his mind, embarrassed by his momentary lapse. He knew the others would have heard.

"We cannot risk whatever, whoever is draining the gems. By closing the portal we believe we can stop the threat. As I said, we need to do it soon."

"Can you send us back to Arcus?" Queen Silvarna asked the only question they really need to know.

"Yes. Although we might need some of the Elders to stay behind."

"Do we have any other choice? What if King Pathanclaw and Pathandon are able to return in the next few days. Can we wait?"

"We cannot take that risk. Besides, King Pathanclaw can meet you on Arcus. He would only be returning here to take you all to Arcus." Ember was very matter of fact about this change in circumstance. *"Ideally, I would wait, but if Queen Silvarna does manage to speak to King Pathanclaw he must know our plans. If they return here, they may well never be able to leave."*

Queen Silvarna nodded, trying to take in this new information. She knew they didn't have long but to leave what had become her home in the next few days; to do this without King Pathanclaw; to arrive on Arcus without the knowledge of how it would be. Would they all still be in danger from whatever ailed them last time? Had time really allayed the fear of the virus or was that even the reason they left? Were there more secrets to be revealed? It was too much. But whatever happened, they would prevail. In her heart, for her heart, and her unborn youngling, it had to work.

She looked to General Bluewing. He would have to make the decision. He would be leading them on Arcus. It was his responsibility to decide their fate and fight the threats. General Bluewing looked her directly in the eye and nodded. They were strong. They would defeat their enemies.

"Queen Silvarna. Please." Ember motioned to a rock in the middle of the cave. Queen Silvarna nodded and after a final look at Bluewing, she flew to the rock. Folding her wings she settled and waited for what would come next.

Ember and Ritikus flew down into the gems below and were joined by the other guardians, Aryalax and Draxonos. Daysong joined Longsong and the ritual began. The gems became brighter and brighter until Bluewing closed his eyes.

Chapter 21 – Arcus

I ronhand parried the sword as it passed within inches of his face. The Keeper laughed as the Master of Sword dodged behind and tapped Ironhand lightly on the backside.

"Attacked with your own iron! Oh the shame," Morbark taunted. He just managed to duck as Ironhand's massive axe cut through the air.

"Take care, Master Sword. He will have your head clean off with one swipe." Valivar looked up from his book, to take in the scene before him.

"I surrender, I surrender," Morbark said, clearly able to fight all day without breaking a sweat.

They all laughed. It was a good feeling, there had been precious little to smile about lately. But everything was coming to fruition and they hoped, soon, to be sailing away to regroup before Prince Villian returned. The moment Prince Villian had disappeared, any final doubts they'd had about magic and the quest had disappeared. Not that Ironhand had doubted, but he normally put his trust in things he saw with his own eyes.

The small group refreshed themselves and sitting back, they relaxed as they enjoyed each other's company. Valivar's thoughts often strayed back to the night Prince Villian had left. The fighting had been fierce and he and Ironhand had tried to help Raykan but there had been too many of them. They'd escaped through one of the secret caves Raykan had made them aware of. When they had come out into the night air, Morbark had found them and taken them to safety deep in the woods. It was beyond the castle patrols and they were safe until they had regrouped.

The day after the Master Sword had returned with Lady Cartina's maid. Ironhand had blushed like a lovesick boy, much to the amusement of Valivar. A plan had been set in motion and they both appreciated the knowledge that Raykan was safe. They'd been shocked when they heard the news that Baynard was alive.

"That toad." Ironhand had smashed his fist on a rock, doing slightly more damage to the rock and Luciana had been unable to hold back a squeak of alarm. Ironhand had apologised profusely, aware of the amusement from the others. It made him scowl, which deepened their mirth.

"I'm shocked to learn he's alive, my lady. He was grievously injured, so much so, he appeared dead when we last saw him."

"We heard a great commotion when the soldiers returned. They carried Baynard into the castle and the next time we saw him, he looked in pain but certainly far from death's door," Lady Cartina's maid confirmed.

This worried the Keeper, clearly magic was involved somehow. But how and who? How had someone been hiding in their midst who was capable of healing someone so grievously wounded?

Discussions over, Luciana had been returned safely to the castle. It had been agreed that she would come alone. They decided if she was found outside the city walls, she could easily say she got lost gathering herbs for her mistress. It was not so easy with the Master of Sword in tow and since someone had been clearly watching Villian all these years, they could not risk being caught.

Late in the day, as Valivar shared the food Ironhand had caught, Morbark having returned to the castle earlier in the day, the smith questioned Valivar about the days of dragons. An air of respect and awe always entered Ironhand's voice when he realised how old his friend really was. It was also no coincidence they were friends. The smith's many times great grandfather had committed himself to the cause, and as such, knowledge was passed through the families, with maybe a little bit being lost or embellished along the way. But as a new generation took over, the Keeper of Books was always moulding the new smith. It felt like a connection to a time gone by.

"Spit it out." The Keeper could almost hear his friend's thoughts. It was interfering with his enjoyment of his dinner.

"Bloody librarians. It's like you can see into my mind and tease out my very thoughts."

"What makes you think I can't?"

Ironhand laughed nervously.

"I feel like I have so many gaps in my knowledge. If we are to make it, then I need to know what came before. I cannot plan for dangers I know nothing about."

The Keeper smiled. He had known teaching this brute of a man to read when he was a boy was a bad idea. The more he learnt, the more questions he'd asked. But that was the way of learning. Valivar took a long drink of his ale and settled his blanket over his shoulders. The temperature was dropping as night took hold.

"You know some of the story, but as storytellers, we usually start at the beginning. Shall we say, Once Upon a Time..."

Ironhand leaned back against a tree trunk and held his goblet in his hand. He harboured a love of stories and the Keeper of Books had a fair few of them he could recall to his mind.

"You know that dragons and humans lived in peace for many thousands of years. The dragons didn't really have that much to do with us and then one day, Raykan and Pathanclaw – who is now King Pathanclaw, formed a friendship. This developed over time and eventually Pathanclaw made the mistake of teaching Raykan a tiny bit of magic. Maybe he was showing off, maybe he wanted to impress Raykan, but it was the catalyst which led to the dragons having to leave."

Valivar took another sip before continuing. Ironhand got up and threw another log on the fire and settled back down, as the sparks flew into the night. They were well hidden and didn't need to worry about being spotted. The stars were the only other witnesses to the story.

"Ironhand nearly choked on his ale. "Raykan has a twin brother? He had, has what?"

"A twin brother. Obviously, no-one remembers him as only myself and Raykan were alive to record these times. He was the opposite to Raykan, cruel, and desperate for power. He is Raykan's one weakness. His twin, Barakar persuaded his brother to teach him magic. Barakar had a thirst, almost a manic obsession, with learning magic. He was the one that created the book. He made his brother help him and in secret they somehow turned the confusing thoughts of magic into words. It was no mean feat. From how Raykan described it to me it's not so much words that are formed but feelings, so how they managed to do this, I do not know. But they did and it was the worst thing they could have done."

Valivar took another sip. He'd spent so long in the library alone his voice wasn't used to the art of conversation. Setting his goblet down he continued, "Raykan betrayed Pathanclaw, Barakar betrayed Raykan and Pathanclaw betrayed his family. It was a mess."

"So how did you get involved and how did you get to live so long?"

"Patience, my friend. All in good time." He grinned. He would make him pay now and Ironhand settled in for the long version. He was getting exactly what he wanted. The long night would go quicker with a long tale to be told. He only wished he had a warm body, and his face flushed at the thought of Luciana.

"Too late they discovered Barakar was planning to kill the dragons so that he could take the magic powers the dragons protected. The only way of stopping the extinction of Arcus was to pretend the dragons had become allergic to humans and the dragons needed to leave Arcus to save their species. Although it wasn't a complete lie, as something ravaged through the dragons. It made the ones left turn on each other. The final battle was a blood bath." Valivar shook his head. He could still hear the screams and smell the dragon blood.

"But why didn't they just burn Barakar to a crisp and be done with it?"

"Barakar had become too powerful by then, and the dragons all believed the lie Pathanclaw had told them. It was too late to turn back. Barakar had been defeated near the end or so they thought. They also thought Barakar may have another copy of the book and we needed to retrieve it in order to destroy written magic once and for all and close the portals."

"But that means destroying everything to do with magic. And what about you and Raykan?"

Valivar nodded. He knew the sacrifice of his life would be required one day and he was ready for it. To hear that his precious library had been destroyed had broken something in him, despite his little friends saving as much as they could. He was tired. He could see now why humans only lived a short time. Living for thousands of years was difficult, especially when you didn't have your friends with you and so many passed over the years. Each death was an open wound, and, like mortal wounds, they festered in the mind.

The friends were silent for a few moments, listening to the wood crackling in the fire.

"The dragons created the Festival of Time at the very

beginning of their history. It was a way of joining worlds and time. Often the dragons left to look after the gem caves which are scattered throughout time and planets. But they closed them when the dragons left Arcus in the hope of stopping Barakar, only allowing them to open once every thousand years in the hope things would change."

"How many were killed during the war?"

"Thousands. I don't know how Barakar did it, but I suppose in a way, the dragons were allergic to humans. Well, one human in particular. Barakar had amassed a great army and trained some of them to do the very basics of magic, but it was enough. The dragons were not expecting the humans to attack. They didn't even know where the attacks came from. It took a while before the dragons took control back and by then, many had turned on each other and the elders were in no doubt they needed to leave the planet and temporarily close the portals until time had healed."

"It's a wonder the dragons will ever trust us again!"

"I know. The cries keep me awake even now. Despite their greatness, it's a lesson to us all that size doesn't matter."

A slight laugh caught in the back of Ironhand's throat, and he started to choke on the large gulp of ale he'd just consumed. He appreciated his friend trying to lighten the mood, but it was very short lived. He tried to comprehend the story. There were so many things he struggled to see in his mind. The image of thousands of dragons for one, the fact that Raykan had been friends with a dragon and between them they had betrayed their own species and caused the death of so many. Even with this knowledge, Ironhand found it hard to feel anger towards Raykan who had certainly suffered for his folly and weakness. He'd had to live for thousands of years, waiting for the right time to put things right between humans and dragons.

"So, how did you end up living for thousands of years then? How is that even possible?"

Valivar sighed, he felt bone weary. To take his mind back so far was a challenge, but he owed Ironhand the truth. He'd believed his tales and he owed this generation of smiths an explanation.

"When it was clear what was happening, I was summoned to a secret meeting with the elders. As I entered, Raykan passed me. His face haunted my thoughts for many years. A broken man who was going to have to relive his misdoings and deceptions for a very long time."

Valivar shifted and pulled the blanket tighter. He took another sip before carrying on with his tale.

"I cannot talk of everything that happened in there, but what I say now has never been told to a human soul until..."

Ironhand raised his hand to silence him. He carefully drew his axe as he squinted into the darkness.

Lady Cartina did her duty as she did every night, only tonight was different because she had to endure her sister. Helendy certainly knew how to shine in company, knew how to manipulate others with a skill a king would be envious of. She worked her way around court, soon finding favour with the highest born.

The crowds parted as Prince Villian's warriors entered the room. The king had asked for a show to entertain the crowds and there was none better, even if Dyana did despise performing.

Dyana walked the line. She was proud of her warriors. She'd handpicked them all. She knew her story was often told in whispers in the streets of Arcus. Others dreamt of what she had become. She'd been visiting the castle with a friend, having come from the fighting pits of the west every few months to trade. This particular day in the market she'd witnessed a man stealing from a vendor. The man had threatened the vendor when challenged and so she'd stepped in. The man sneered at her and told her to take her long legs and pretty face elsewhere. Moments later he was face down in the dirt, eating his words, much to the delight of the crowd. Prince Villian had been visiting Ironhand and had approached her. His forthright address had impressed her.

"That was impressive."

"Thank you, boy. I'm glad you were entertained." She bowed low to him, as a few people clapped in the crowd.

Her sister, Lanu leaned in close, "That's not a boy. That's Prince Villian of Arcus."

Dyana raised her eyebrow as the boy smiled at her, seemingly not bothered she had called him boy. She folded her arms and looked him up and down. His clothes were made of the finest material coin could buy, the stitching better than anything she had ever seen. He was still staring at her, a wry smile on his face. He couldn't be more than eight she thought but acted as if he were full grown.

"A Prince? What would a prince be doing out here without his royal guard?"

"A prince often comes here without his guard. Why would I need a guard to walk amongst my own people? Besides, I can defend myself."

Dyana arched her well used eyebrow again, "You can, can you?"

"Dyana." Her sister warned, "this isn't a good idea. He's the Prince."

"Well, it sounded like he was challenging me, and you know I never turn down a challenge. What does everyone think?"

By now a big crowd had gathered around them, shouts

encouraged them to fight. Dyana knew how to work a crowd into a frenzy, it was why she was Queen of the fighting pits and untouchable by the owners of the pits. She was guaranteed to bring in plenty of coin to grease their filthy palms.

"How about it, Prince. Fancy a fight?"

"My Master sword said I should practice every day. You can be my practice for today. My Lady." Prince said with a bow which equalled her own in style and arrogance.

Dyana laughed loudly and pointed at the prince, "I like you. Choose your weapon, my Prince."

Prince Villian looked around the market.

"I choose," he paused for effect, as Dyana realised she wasn't the only one who could work a crowd, "wooden spoons."

There was silence and then the crowd erupted into laughter.

Dyana's stony face met the princes as the crowd laughed around them. She placed her hands together and bowed, "Spoons it is, my Prince."

He was grinning as she raised her head. Moments later they were both laughing as they moved to pick up their spoons the vendor had happily lent them. They circled each other intently, spoons held like their swords. Before they could advance, the royal guard arrived and quickly set about dispersing the crowd.

"Sorry, looks like our fun has been brought to an end. Until another day."

"Of course, my Prince. I look forward to it." Dyana raised her spoon and bowed her head.

The prince turned and returned to the castle with his guard. As Dyana and Lanu were finishing up their business in the market, a guard found her and gave her an invitation.

"What's it say?" Lanu asked, as she secured her pack, ready to leave.

"We have been invited to a meeting at the castle with the prince tomorrow. He has something he wishes to discuss."

"Are you going to go?"

"Of course, I am. Who would miss the chance of seeing inside the castle? They will probably offer us some good food!"

"Always thinking about food, sister."

"You know me."

The next day they had made their way to the castle. Living in the streets, they had never been in a place so grand. Lanu kept elbowing her in the side until Dyana threatened her sister. Dyana straightened her back as they were led through the large rooms. They expected to be taken to the hall but they were led through into a large, enclosed training ground. A man was waiting in the middle. The guards left them and closed the doors behind them.

Dyana's hand strayed to the empty sword scabbard – their weapon had been taken on entry. The man in front of her smiled as he noticed her reflexes.

"Sorry I'm late. Princely things to do."

The boy came bounding through the corridor in high spirits. He stopped and bowed to the man before him, remembering his manners.

"Sorry, Master of Sword, may I introduce Dyana and Lanu."

Dyana was shocked he knew their names but didn't show it.

With his hand behind his back the Master circled them both. They moved as if they were shadow dancing and maintained eye contact with him. The sisters knew each other's every move. They had fought back-to-back many times. The prince threw them each a practice sword.

"Is this some kind of joke?" Dyana said to the grinning

Prince, thinking surely, they didn't bring them here just to kill them. Maybe her rudeness would cost them their lives. But he was a child, and she wasn't usually wrong about people. He didn't seem to follow in his father's ruthless footsteps.

"Not a joke. A test." The Master Sword said, as he raised his practice sword. "You up for a fight or are you scared?"

Dyana's smile gave him his answer. Her sister raised her sword and they attacked as one.

As the sun started to drop low in the sky they finally stopped, "Well, that was some fight. I think we will call it a draw."

Dyana was too busy drinking to argue. The Master of Sword had them on the run for most of the fight. They both had moves the other had never seen, his learned through discipline and training and hers, through survival of the fittest. They had all learned something new that day.

"Please, follow me," the young Prince said, as they finished their drinks.

He led them into a chamber next to the training room, the sisters fell on the table and started to eat without invitation. The fighting had made them ravenous. When they'd eaten their fill, Dyana said, "What is all this about?"

Morbark answered, "My Prince would like to have his own warriors who are loyal to him. He respectfully asks that you two are the first and lead his warriors. You will be paid well and will be free to recruit your own warriors, with my help and final approval, of course. But you must live in the castle and train with us. Your fighting pit days must come to an end."

Lanu's mouth had dropped open and only pride stopped Dyana's from doing the same. In her experience, when something was too good to be true, it usually was.

"What's the catch and why us?"

"There is no catch. Prince Villian wants this, and we

will make it so. If not you, then we will find others. But I doubt we will find any as good. Today was your test and you passed with flying colours."

Dyana eyed him to see if he was paying compliments to curry favour but his praise seemed genuine. What a strange turn of events. They had come here for supplies and now they were being offered this. She turned to Prince Villian.

"You don't seem the kind of person to let others do your talking for you. Why do you want us?"

The young Prince faced her like an adult. In her life, children had always had to grow up sooner than they should. She wouldn't admit it to her sister but one thing she loved about the castle was seeing the young children at play. They were allowed to avoid the harshness of growing up too early and she envied them. It seemed the young Prince, despite his birth right, had been also made to give up something precious. He spoke like a man.

"I read in a book once that women fighters were the fiercest and most loyal warriors. When one day I go into battle, I want the element of surprise. You will be my surprise."

It was cunning, childlike and also like a prince. What he thought and wanted could come true. Was she going to give him his wish? Did she want herself and her sister to be warriors to this future king? To protect and guard him with their lives? She knew the answer and didn't need to ask her sister. "We would be honoured to serve you and become your warriors. Who am I to deny a Prince his every desire?" She ended with a wry smile and another bow.

"Out of interest, what if we'd said no?" Dyana asked as she faced Prince Villian.

"I would have been very offended and probably asked Master Sword to chop your heads off and throw them off the battlements as a warning to all my subjects who do not grant my every wish."

Dyana picked up a ripe fruit from the table and threw it at him. It hit him in the chest, and at first, he looked shocked. She felt Morbark move slightly, but the young prince laughed, a young and innocent sound and returned the fruit with vigour. He had a good aim. What was life without a little fun, after all.

Now Dyana signalled to her warriors in the great hall and the show began. How she hated performing, but she was used to playing a part.

Chapter 22 – Luminosa

Pathanclaw watched as the humans guarding the female dragons moved up and down the line. The guards were oblivious to their presence. Each crack of a whip on a dragon sent a wave of pain through him, even though he knew they wouldn't be able to feel it though their thick scales. It was what it represented. The humans had power over the dragons, they were not equal, and the humans were not scared of the dragons. He wouldn't wish for the humans to be scared but a healthy respect was always in order when something was many times your size and could breathe fire, or so Raykan had always pointed out.

"Shall we do something?" Pathandon asked.

"No, not yet. We need to wait."

"Wait for what?"

He could hear the impatience in his grandson and sympathised. Everything in his being wanted to swoop down and burn them to a crisp, to teach them what they were doing was wrong. But he saw the glee in their faces. They were not doing this because they had to, it was because they liked it.

"Pathanclaw, can you hear me?"

Pathanclaw couldn't hide his surprise, *"Silvarna?"*

"Grandmother?"

So, Pathandon could hear her too. Maybe it was a trick the Masters were playing. He scanned the horizon but there was no sign of them yet.

"Silvarna," he said again. Not believing his heart could

speak to him from so far away. But the voice was hers, the love in her voice unmistakable. *"My heart. Is everything okay? How are you doing this?"*

"It's the guardians' of gems. We don't have much time. I need to tell you the gems are being stolen from Suntra. Something is stealing their power and the Elders insist we must leave. We will meet you on Arcus, my love."

They could hardly take it in. How could something be stealing the power from the gem cave on Suntra? The dragons were linked in a way which not many could understand. How could they use the power of the gems so far away? Only dragons could harness the power, or so they thought.

Pathanclaw and Pathandon's eyes met, and they both focused on the dragons. Were the Masters stealing the power of the gems through the dragons here? Pathanclaw had never thought of it but knew it must be possible.

"Pathanclaw, can you still hear me?"

"Yes, my love. Sorry. You are sure? When will you leave?"

"Yes, the guardian said it is not being used by the dragons here. Does this help you? In two days. I must go now."

"It does. Thank you, my love, and the guardians. How are you all?"

"We are safe. I'm sorry about General Battlewing."

All their hearts were heavy at the thought. *"The new general Bluewing is a worthy replacement,"* Silvana added.

This made their emotions flare with a mixture of sadness and joy.

"I have to go now, my heart. It's fading here. I must go. Quickly, tell me, will you meet us on Arcus?"

Pathanclaw could hear the strain in her voice. He wanted to say so much, wanted to listen to her for hours and fly to their cave and it just be them, entwined, with no cares and no responsibilities.

"We are well, Grandmother. Please tell Bluewing I miss him." Pathandon answered for them so his grandfather could gather himself.

"I will. I have to go. I love you both."

"We will meet you on Arcus in a few days. We have found the humans. The one I sought. We have the females, Silvarna. We have them." Pathanclaw hoped she'd heard him.

Silvarna disappeared from their minds and Pathanclaw hoped she was alright. He couldn't imagine the strain of connecting with them so far away. He tried to reconnect with her mind but she was lost to him once again. He sighed.

As Pathanclaw and his grandson wondered about the gems. Two Masters walked out from the forest, the children and their creatures following in their wake. But King Pathanclaw's keen eyes saw some of the younglings blend back into the forest. Were they escaping? He broke his silence and warned Thanan and prince Villian before rising into the air as Barakar spoke.

As Thanan and Villian moved cautiously towards the clearing, Thanan couldn't believe how quiet it was. There was always some sound in the camp. The noise from the children who had recently acquired their creature meant it was rarely silent. The worst was when the new children arrived, and their cries disturbed his sleep in the middle of the night. Everyone ended up grumpy for weeks through lack of sleep. But none of the children who had been their years could hold it against the newcomers, it had happened to all of them.

Villian was in awe of the size of the trees as they moved past the camp and into the forest. Thanan pointed out the lantern trees as they moved quietly. Villian felt as if he would fall over, straining his neck to see the lanterns that almost touched the sky. The strange colour of the sky transfixed him, and he reluctantly turned his eyes back on Thanan.

Villian twisted the ring from his betrothed. He wondered as he so often did, since the day he had left, how she was faring. For the thousandth time his thoughts turned to Raykan, Ironhand and the Keeper. His hope that they were alive and well on Arcus, that somehow, they had escaped the attackers. Villian knew the men sent to kill him could have only come from his father, although he couldn't accept that his father would try and kill him, but Baynard was his father's hand. Could the king really have wanted his only son dead? His new wife had not produced an heir, which had always guaranteed Villian's safety. He wondered if that had changed. They had a mission to complete. But he wondered how Raykan had managed to get hold of his light, they had nothing like this on Arcus. Could there be a place like this on Arcus, or was Raykan able to move between worlds and time? But then wouldn't he have been able to do this without waiting for the one to come along, for him to come along and try to change the fortune of their world? Couldn't they have all found each other before now? The constant disjoined thoughts gave him a headache and he tried to set his thoughts aside.

Thanan signalled for Villian to stop. Villian felt grateful, his mind was wandering and not as focused as it should be. Thanan pointed through the trees and Villian could make out a shape. The cave lay straight ahead, as they waited to assess any danger, they saw a shadow move towards the cave entrance.

"It's Triana," Thanan hissed as quietly as he could. Villian could feel his friend stiffen and put his hand on his arm but an electric shock made his remove it swiftly.

"Thanan," he warned. Thanan relaxed slightly.

"We have to go. Star is in there."

"Okay, let's just wait and make sure that its only her."

Thanan nodded but it felt as if they waited an age before Villian moved forward, his sword glinting in the red sky. Thanan breathed in and out, trying to slow his emotions and make his mind ready. If he needed to form magic, then he needed to be calm. Tobias always made him breathe until he'd found his place. Quickly those remembered lessons made him relax. He followed Villian, scared of what they might find.

Villian turned, nodded and they moved quickly now, eager to get Star and Dragon to safety. They heard a scream and all other thoughts of danger left them as they ran into the cave. As they turned the corner, they spotted the cages at the back and Triana standing in front of one. Her hands were red, blasting fire balls into the cage. Thanan could see Star's prone form cowering, but he couldn't quite make sense of the scene, as the fire didn't seem to be touching her.

Triana was so focused on her victim, she didn't see them. Villian dropped his sword and ran into Triana catching her around the middle and pushing her to the floor. The fire ball stopped instantly, as a sickening thud reach Thanan's ears. He felt relief when he saw Villian stand up but Triana was deathly white, as a pool of blood formed where her head had stuck a rock.

Thanan kicked the door open easily, the heat of Triana's fireballs had melted the lock. He moved to Star's body not daring to believe she could be alive. Star didn't know magic, she couldn't have formed a protective spell. He wished he hadn't glanced into the cage next to her. He almost didn't recognise Dragon. Her striking blue colour had been replaced by blistered grey scales. Her eyes were fixed on Star to the last.

Thanan felt the tears fall unchecked down his face.

As soon as the children started walking into the clearing with the Masters, Pathanclaw fixed his mind on the girl who was chained up. They had looked on in shock as the children had been first marched into the plain in front of the dragons and then twenty of the children, Pathandon had counted, had dragons of their own. They were not big like Star's Dragon had become. Some of the children had magical creatures but they were only lizards. Would they become dragons or stay as they were?

"Can you hear me? Do not be alarmed or cry out."

The girl didn't make a sound but he could feel the emotions running through her. It reminded him of Star. He wondered how they were, but couldn't spare the time. He needed to figure out how to save the dragons and the children.

"Who are you?" The girl sounded scared but challenging. She was a fighter. A good sign.

"That is no matter for now. Just know we are here to save you. Do you have any influence over the other children?"

"Yes, a little. But it's difficult to do anything. I'm tied up, but I will get myself free."

Pathanclaw was impressed by how quickly she adapted. He always found adults underestimated what their younglings were capable off. In his experience, they were often more balanced than the adults.

"The boy. Can he help?"

"Yes."

"When I tell you, I need all the children to run behind the dragons. Do you understand?"

"Yes. We will be ready."

"Thank you. It will not be long."

Whilst the dragon had been talking, a range of

thoughts had moved at lightning speed through Kyla's mind. Could this be the Masters playing tricks? She didn't think so. The dragons who had come through the portal were here to save the children and they had to do everything to help them rescue them. No matter the cost. They might only get one chance. She met Galan's eye again, trying to convey her thoughts.

As the children settled their creatures, the Master moved down the line of children issuing instructions. The spell casters were to form fireballs and the ones with creatures were to have their dragons ready to fire at the enemy. Galan couldn't see how they could be any better than the Masters using their power. But Kyla said using magic drained their energy quickly. Maybe the Masters wanted to expend their energy first.

There was a glint far off and Galan's eyes sought the speck in the distance. It came closer and closer and soon one of the great red dragons came into view. It was majestic, so graceful in the sky as it glided effortlessly, one small beat of its giant wings, propelling forward. It landed some distance away. Galan wondered where the other one was.

Galan felt as if everyone was holding their breath. He heard a noise from one the dragons behind him and braved a look. It was also a red dragon. Maybe it was part of this new dragon's pack. If Galan knew what a sad but hopeful dragon looked like, he would swear it was looking back at him. The dragon tore its eyes away from its kin and looked at him, its head tilting slightly, making the chains churn up the black sand which was all around. Galan smiled, he couldn't help himself. A real dragon.

Pathanclaw looked out over the scene before him. Seven hooded Masters were flanked by a long row of children who stood between him and his kin. His eyes found Ruby, one of the females Pathanclaw had once hoped would be the bearer of his grandson's children, the ones to continue the royal red dragons. In his conversations with Raykan it had amused him when they'd inevitably turned onto the subject of 'couples' as the humans called them. Raykan was shocked that sometimes the females were hundreds of years older than their mate and they would mate for life when they had chosen each other. Pathanclaw had replied that he thought it odd the royal humans decided who their children were going to marry. Pathanclaw had hopes but it was always the individual's choice. It should be their decision. But then Pathanclaw couldn't argue with Prince Villian and his Lady Cartina, the boy seemed very struck with her.

There was a guard standing at the end of the row of dragons nearest the forest. The Masters obviously had confidence the dragons could not get out of the hideous contraptions which weighed them to the ground. Pathanclaw did not look towards the two figures who were making their way towards the unsuspecting guard.

Star felt them lift her and she saw Triana, pale and limp on the floor. She wasn't capable of feeling joy, sadness or anger, she felt nothing. She turned her head and her eyes met Villian's. She wondered why he was crying. She couldn't imagine what had happened to make a Prince cry. Then she turned her head and wished she hadn't. The beautiful warm eyes of Dragon no longer shone. Dragon was dead. Star's soul broke.

Chapter 23 – Suntra

Queen Silvarna felt a sensation she had never felt before. It was as if she was something more than she was. Not a dragon, but everything. There was nothing she couldn't see or do. She was part of everything.

General Bluewing looked on as the dragons surrounded his queen. He could see the giant grey scar in the gem cave growing bigger. How much power were they using? It was only a fraction of the gems in cave, but still the dragons were much fewer in number now. It would take thousands of years for them to replenish the gems. He doubted they had made the right decision to do this. What benefit could this be to the King? But at the same time he was desperate to know how his friend was and when they were coming back. He hoped it would be soon.

He tried to focus on what was happening. His mind was reeling from the news they would have to leave in the next few days. He knew the younglings were as ready as they could be. But was he ready? Could he command them like his father? Would he be worthy of being the general? He set it to one side and concentrated. There would be time afterwards to plan their departure.

The very air felt electric. Was it working? Was she able to speak with his grandfather and friend? He couldn't tell, couldn't hear his queen's thoughts. Moments later the other dragons moved away and Queen Silvarna fell off the giant rock outcrop and onto the gems below.

Chapter 24 – Arcus

Dyana's eyes never left Lady Cartina. She could see the lady did not share the love of her sister as she did. The air between them crackled with disdain. It still annoyed her that she had been duped by Prince Villian. He had sent them away to train in the mountains and on their return all hell had broken loose as she found out he had disappeared. As soon as she'd arrived back in the castle she had been summoned by the King. Her cheeks flamed at the disrespect he'd shown them. Where were the prince's famous warriors when they were needed? Morbark had filled her in after her dressing down. She understood they would have been in danger if the prince had told her his plans. Still, it stung that he hadn't confided his secrets to her, but she acknowledged she would have stopped him. They couldn't have gone with him and he needed her here for when he returned. Her warriors would be ready.

Lady Cartina caught her eye and Dyana nodded. They had agreed a signal but it was too dangerous to talk here. There could be no connection between them. Lady Cartina needed to remain innocent of any knowledge of what was about to happen.

Show done, Dyana and her warriors left the great hall. She needed to wash and get the stink off her body, the smell of wealth and entitlement, the stench of privilege and ignorance. Did they not know what was happening? She would be glad to leave this place. Once Prince Villian had left, she had felt threats from every corner. She stalked down the corridor, the walls held so many memories.

The challenge to recruit her own warriors by Prince Villian had not taken long. Six months after it, she had her warriors. They had travelled far and wide to find the right women to take on this task. Dyana had a brutal training regime for them and had insisted her warriors were housed near the prince. It had caused uproar in the royal house as others in the household were moved but the heir to the throne got what he wanted, and the sisters soon found out that this young prince usually got his own way. They trained with the prince everyday and discovered he was a fast learner. Dyana also felt the women would fight harder if they respected and loved their champion. It had been Dyana who suggested the summer games. They'd fought and played hard for honour and trophies and not for their lives as she had. She was unbeaten in most games, which did not make her popular with many of the men, especially Baynard. The first year he had entered thinking he would be victorious. She'd made sure she'd beaten him in every game. She knew she'd made an enemy of him, but she had seen how he treated Prince Villian and it gave her great pleasure.

Dyana whispered to Lanu and she left to seek Luciana. Dyana hoped no bad news would reach her. It was worrying that Helendy had joined the rest of the family. It showed the king did not trust them and everyone knew it. There was an uneasy feeling as she made her way to her room for the final time under the reign of this king. They would be leaving and she doubted the same royal would be seated on throne when they returned.

Chapter 25 – Luminosa

"How are we going to get her in the boat?" Thanan asked. He looked at Villian and imagined he looked the same, tear-streaked, dirty, and pale so that he almost couldn't look at Villian. He glanced down at Star. She'd fainted when she had seen Dragon in the cage. Dragon had somehow taken the damage from Star onto herself. But how? Dragon had made the ultimate sacrifice for Star.

Thanan and Villian had heard nothing more from Pathanclaw and Pathandon. They wondered how the dragons were faring. Would they be able to save the children? Thanan and Villian knew they had to focus on getting Star to safety. Thanan hoped Pol would be able to help his friend. But would she ever recover from losing Dragon? Would his best friend no longer be the same? He swallowed the lump in his throat as they reached the entrance to the cave and slowly made their way to the boat. Villian was carrying Star over his shoulder and was dripping with sweat.

He lay Star carefully onto the floor and Thanan moved into the boat. Between them they manoeuvred Star into the bottom of the boat. Villian took off his jacket and gave it to Thanan, who placed it under her head. She was unnaturally pale, her normally dark skin was pale and if not for the slight rise and fall of her chest, he would have thought the worst. Thanan reached over and moved her long blue hair off her face, a few strands defying his touch. He smiled, even her hair was stubborn. He hoped she would be okay.

Thanan opened his mind and told Pol what had happened. He felt the sadness mirror his.

"Once you have pulled Star through, keep the boat there. Villian and I are going to help the children. Pathanclaw said they are on their way."

Triana woke, her head pounding. Sitting up slowly, she looked around. Star was gone. All she remembered was being hit by something. Star's friends must have come to rescue her. Triana grabbed hold of the cage and pulled herself up. Dizziness washed over her and she felt sick. She wiped away a trickle of blood and let her body settle before opening her eyes again.

Dead eyes stared back at her. At first she couldn't work out what see was seeing and then she realised it was Star's dragon. But it had no colour, it looked like solid dust. Tears she hadn't welcomed, fell down her cheeks. She had done this. She didn't know why she'd become so angry, why she had vented it on Star. But Dragon must have died instead. Unless Star was dead as well and they could only carry her body and they had left Dragon. With shaking hands, she reached into the cage and as the tip of her finger found Dragon, its body disintegrated like dust.

Triana turned her head as the dust settled. Reaching inside the cage she picked up four bright blue gems. They were a heavy weight of guilt in her palm, judging her actions. What had she done? How could she do this? What had she become? She'd only agreed to help the Masters because they said she wouldn't disappear when the time came. They would train her to be a Master, but is this what she would have to do? She ripped the talisman from her neck, the talisman which was like a beacon. It was how the Masters knew they were coming back. It gave her extra power, it had changed her. She was angry all the time. She hated everyone and everything. It was cursed. She flung it down on the floor and as she gripped the gems a blue light came from her hands and she watched as the talisman melted at her feet. She sank to the floor once again, relief washing over her. Her small body curled up and she sobbed.

Chapter 26 – Suntra

Bluewing flew down and settled next to the queen. She couldn't be dead. Not Queen Silvarna. But he quickly realised she was still alive. She was breathing and he relaxed. The world seemed to be fraught with dangers ever since King Pathanclaw and Pathandon had left. More than once he'd wished his father were alive and in charge., that they had decided to stay on Suntra and he and Pathandon could go back to pretending to be adults. The real truth of being the General was not what he'd expected.

"She will be well, General. She just needs to rest for a few hours. Queen Silvarna is strong. She has survived."

Bluewing thought he heard Ember's words tail off to the end. *'We didn't think she would.'*

Bluewing looked to Ember. The other dragons had left, no doubt to rest and recover. Despite the news about their imminent departure, he didn't want to put the plans into motion until he'd spoken to Queen Silvarna. There might be information they needed. King Pathanclaw could have insisted they wait for him. He settled, knowing he would need to wait. The hardest thing to do.

"Do you not mind staying behind?" Bluewing asked, wondering if the reclusive black dragon was welcoming this unusual interaction with him. He and Pathandon had discussed the black and green dragons on many occasions, often wishing they had been born the protectors of the gems. The purple dragons were even more elusive.

"*I consider it my duty, General Bluewing.*" Bluewing thought that was the end of the conversation and he settled to wait for Queen Silvarna to wake. He felt a powerful energy in the cave and marvelled at the gems, the power of which could send dragons and humans across time, to other planets. He and Pathandon had wondered how many gems had been used during the big battle when the dragons had left. Rumours were that the dragons had not only become allergic to humans but dragons had been compelled to attack each other. He realised his mind was not closed to others, as he looked up, he saw Ember staring at him.

"*I hope it is something you never see again, General Bluewing. We all hope you return to the peace and harmony which surrounded our kind for countless millennia. They say the world cannot stay the same, but to have such a devasting attack...*" Ember stopped, clearly overwhelmed by the feeling.

Bluewing felt the emotions keenly and watched over his Queen, hoping she would wake. They must leave, and he must lead them but would he be able to leave Queen Silvarna behind if she didn't wake?

Chapter 27 – Arcus

"**I**t's only me. It was silly to think I could creep up on you."

Raykan came through the dark wood, leaning heavily on his staff. His body and mind were weary. The last few days had been taxing and time spent on a stone-cold floor hadn't helped. He missed his hut. A fleeting sadness passed through him because he had no doubt Baynard had burnt it down. No matter, it was just a place, but his chair had been comfortable and he missed his brews which had helped to keep the pain at bay.

Valivar rose, thinking his friend could have easily killed them. Making a noise had been deliberate. With that staff and limp, they would have heard anyone else from a long way away. Ironhand stood and put out his hand, avoiding giving his familiar bear hug due to the fire scars that covered Raykan's body. They clasped hands and Raykan turned to nod at Valivar.

Raykan moved slowly and turned to sit onto a log, a deep sigh emerging as he settled. It had been a long trek from the castle and he'd taken time out to wash in a river when he had emerged from the filth. The smell still clung to him but it was an improvement, although he thought he saw his friends avoid a deep breath when they were downwind of him.

"We don't have long before they will come looking for me. Are all the plans still in place?"

Valivar filled him in on the plans whilst Ironhand poured Raykan a well-needed goblet of ale. Ironhand lifted a huge log and settled it on the fire as sparks danced once again into the night. Valivar and Raykan eyed each other, both marvelling at the strength of their friend.

"You were saying there was something you hadn't told anyone, Valivar. I will not compel you to say more than you are inclined but we are far beyond the damage which secrets cause and it may help us to see a path which is unclear to us."

Valivar nodded. He'd already decided to be candid.

"As I said, I will not talk about some of the events, for some are not secrets and have no relevance to our future story. But after you left all those thousands of years ago, the elders formed a plan which I had no choice but to agree with. I hope our friendship is not affected by what I have to tell you?"

"How could I judge you after what I have done? Even though my intentions were not to cause harm and I was fooled by a brother's love, so I would be the first to forgive any indiscretions. No, that is not right. I would not even presume to judge my friend."

Valivar nodded. "The elders knew it would take generations for mistrust and blame to diminish between dragons and humans and they made the mistake of thinking they knew humans. Even after all that had happened, I was given the option of living a long life in exchange for my help. What man reaching the twilight of his life wouldn't want to live longer?"

"You just thought about all the extra books you could read."

Valivar 's smile showed his agreement with Ironhand's statement. "Well, I won't say that realisation didn't inform my decision. But I've discovered there will never be enough time to read all the books I desire. Even in a million lifetimes it wouldn't be possible. I wish I'd realised this sooner."

They all shared a chuckle. Valivar sighed, to hear so

many of his books had been destroyed had taken a little piece of his heart. He was pleased he'd had the forethought to hide some of the most precious books. The children he employed were more than capable of moving in the shadows and they were loyal.

"For the reward of a longer life I was asked to create a myth, a story and weave it into the fabric of society. It was easy to do of course. I had the time after all to leave the hints, to create a book of my own, to set the seed and history that the one would be born and with him came the hope of redemption for dragons and humans."

A sharp intake of breath from Raykan made him tear his gaze away from the fire. He had deceived his friend for so long, yet he had always hoped one day he would get to the tell the truth. He knew his relief at the telling was causing pain for another, but that was the way of secrets. There was rarely a winner.

"So, there was no truth in Prince Villian being the one and the Festival of Time portals being open for them to save Arcus?" Ironhand said disbelievingly.

"The elders wanted to govern the time that dragons and humans came back together. They didn't want anyone to know the mistakes which had been made in allowing humans to learn the magic of the dragons. I created the book under strict supervision, although I wasn't quite sure the dragons could understand our language and us theirs."

It was Raykan turn to sigh. "I've spent so long convincing myself the legacy was real, making myself believe that once the one was found, peace would return to Arcus and Pathanclaw and I could at least return Arcus to what it once was. Deep down I think I knew it was no coincidence. Not that we ever thought or wanted to be forgiven, but it would be something."

"I think you've punished yourself long enough, my friend."

Ironhand lent forward, an edge to his voice, "So, Prince Villian isn't the one? The Quest was a lie? We have sent a young boy to his peril for no reason. Made him believe his life has more meaning than it has, possibly making him reckless? You have not only lied to Raykan but to me. You have, in turn, made me deceive one of my friends."

Ironhand stood up, his face furious and hands clenched. Valivar had miscalculated the one who would be most affected by his revelations.

Valivar held up his hands, palm upwards, "I'm sorry, but I had no choice. I'm sorry I didn't acknowledge your involvement in my deceit but I had no other option. It had to be kept a secret. I made a promise to the elders and I trusted their plan would work. I hope you can forgive me. I did what I thought was best for everyone and knowing Prince Villian, prophecy or not, he would have left anyway to save his people."

Ironhand still looked angry but he nodded. "Yes, I suppose you're right. He's one of the bravest lads I know and maybe without our guidance this day would not have come about. It's a lot to ask of a friendship but I think I have big enough shoulders to bear it."

Valivar nodded, grateful for his quick forgiveness, "Thank you, Ironhand. I cannot tell you what a relief it is to have finally revealed the truth. Secrets take their toll in so many ways. The deceit of a friend is perhaps the worst."

"You should be called the Keeper of Secrets and not the Keeper of Books," Raykan scoffed.

They joined in a strained but welcome chuckle, which eased the words between them and their friendship settled back into place with this new knowledge reconciled.

"So, what was the book you gave Prince Villian before he left?" Raykan said.

"I thought you were too busy creating that portal to notice," Valivar said, surprised.

Raykan's wry smile said he didn't miss anything.

"It was the second book I created for the elders. Even I don't know what it is for. When I'd finished scribing it, they performed some magic which made the words unreadable to my eyes and try as I might, the words have never appeared to me. Put simply, I cannot recall the words I scribed. Someone else was given the knowledge of this."

"More bloody secrets, those elders are just as bad. Doesn't anyone learn any lessons from the past?" Ironhand said, his temper still sitting beneath the surface. It would take a while for this news to be absorbed despite their acceptance that Valivar had little choice. They doubted they would have done differently in his situation. They were all quiet, contemplating the part they had played throughout time.

Finally, Raykan spoke.

"I need to think about the implications of your truths, Valivar. I too, feel as if I have sent the boy to an unknown future, although it gives me hope that the Elders passed something to him. They clearly had a plan, even if they did embellish the prophecy, and their goal is the same. We must hold on to it and hope Prince Villian has found Pathanclaw and they will return to Arcus. For now, I am bone weary and tomorrow we must leave these lands until they return. I beg we get some sleep. We will have plenty of time for talk in the months to come."

The company nodded. Ironhand collected spare blankets and laid them against a tree, although he knew Raykan rarely lay down to sleep. Raykan smiled and grateful settled back against the tree, the most comfortable he'd been in a while. Every part of his body ached but thankfully, sleep came quickly.

Lucinda had spoken to Prince Villian's guards. Apparently one of them was related to her sister. It constantly surprised Lady Cartina how many people Lucinda knew. Despite Prince Villian's disappearance, a guard had been posted to his private chambers. As she walked towards her betrothed's room, she felt nervous about being in his private chamber without him. It seemed a betrayal of his privacy but she felt it was the only way to know him better.

The guard had winked at her as he unlocked the door. It had made her blush, but it was kindly meant. She knew from Lucinda that his guard had been devasted when Prince Villian had disappeared and questions had been asked of him. But Prince Villian had never allowed an escort to accompany him throughout his daily life, so the punishment he'd been given was to spend his days guarding an empty chamber.

Lady Cartina placed her hands behind her and laid them against the solid wooden doors thinking about the times Villian must have touched this very door, the times he'd returned from his secret meetings with Raykan, his teaching with The Keeper and training with the Master Sword and his warriors. His secrets he had held close, never revealing them, and she suspected he wouldn't want to put anyone in danger. If he had any flaws, she was unable to find them.

Large windows dominated the expansive room. The floor to ceiling bookshelves afforded no gaps, and she allowed herself the little time she had to run her hand over them. Her sister would sneer at her, never one for romance. Lady Cartina would admit she was the one for fairy tales. Her daydreams were always of her future. It had always been expected she would marry the heir to the throne as it was her destiny and her duty being the eldest sister of a great house and so far she'd spent her life working towards that goal. She would be the best queen when the time came. Her wish had come true meeting

Prince Villian and knowing he shared her love of Arcus. They would rule in the right way. Or she hoped they would. Did all kings and queens start with good intentions? Doubts had been creeping in during the early hours when sleep eluded her.

She moved her hand and picked up a small painting of Villian's mother. It was stunning and she could see Villian in her image. She felt sorry for this mother who had left her child too soon. If only she could have lived to feel the pride in her son. Prince Villian had been brought up and moulded by people not of his blood. People that believed in the prophecy she had come to learn about and remained true to his mother's wishes and dreams. They were family, and now they were hers. She would help Villian's family.

She continued her slow walk through the room, lightly touching objects and feeling his presence more and more. She opened one of the doors and a light breeze tugged at her hair as the sight, sounds and smells of the castle assaulted her senses as she looked over the balcony.

How many times had Villian stood here, smoothed his hands over the stone and looked out, thinking about his destiny and if he was making the right choices? Had he ever doubted what he was supposed to do and what he was doing? Without the guidance of his parents, he was driven to the goal of saving Arcus and its people and to bring dragons back. Were the old stories really true? She would have liked to have asked Raykan many questions about who he was. She heard all the rumours through court and her maids.

Her eyes looked into the distance. She could just see the darkening of the clouds above the mountains and the huge ridge of dormant volcanoes far, far, into the distance. The threat was ever present. She wondered why the king didn't just order his army to attack and surprise whatever, or whoever, it was. She had asked her father and he'd laughed at her saying young girls shouldn't concern themselves with things they didn't understand. It had annoyed her, but she'd kept quiet. It was better if they thought she didn't worry herself with such things.

The sound of clashing swords and spears made her skirts rustle as she moved to the end of the stone balcony. She reached out and peered over to the training ground of Villian's warriors. Her jaw dropped as she watched them, the muscles straining and flexing, the women grunting as they attacked without mercy. Their display in the hall had been magnificent. They were fierce and her hand clenched at the thought of a sword in her hand. The metal would seem strange as she had never held so much as a dagger, never mind the huge swords and spears Villian's warriors wielded. She didn't want to be seen here, so she moved back into the room, the grunts of the warriors silenced as she closed the doors. Her hand lingered on the ornate handle, worn to one side from the many years of use.

The bed stood imposing and suggestive in the middle of the bedroom. She blushed as she thought of the tales the girls had told growing up. It wasn't fit for a lady's ears, but the ladies in court were often the worst. Lady Cartina made a decision and perched on the end of the bed, her hand shaking slightly as she touched the pillow. The nights Prince Villian laid here, wide awake, thinking about the great deeds he would do and the last night before he left, she hoped, the last night he'd been thinking about her. She opened the drawer next to the bed and inside was a glass perfume bottle, simple and elegant, a thin silver band fitted around the top. Her finger traced the name of Villian's mother, Maya. Carefully she opened the half full bottle. She was surprised by the heavy rose scent which assailed her nostrils. Surely this couldn't have lasted all this time. It smelt so fresh. Lightly, she placed her finger on the rim and dipped it carefully into the bottle. Lifting her finger, she dabbed it gently on her neck. Would Villian be angry with her for doing so? But it made her feel as if she knew his mother. Her scent spoke of freshness, summer days, lightness and happiness. Could a scent really tell you so much about a person? She put the lid back on, placed it carefully back in the drawer and closed it.

A quiet tap on the door made her breath quicken. A signal. Someone was coming. Her heart raced as she looked around for somewhere to hide. The heavy floor to ceiling drapes seemed her only option. She rose quickly, smoothed down the cover, tiptoed behind the curtain, making sure her feet were concealed. The curtain reached around and she found a little hidden seat set inside the large window frame. She pulled her knees up to her chest and tried to calm her breathing as the door to the prince's room opened.

Chapter 28 – Luminosa

Thanan hadn't discussed it with Villian, but he knew they couldn't leave the children to their fate. They would probably be scared of the dragons. The only person they knew was Thanan, so he had to be there to make them come with them. Whilst the Masters had them, it would make it hard for the dragons to act. They wouldn't risk hurting the children. His thoughts went to Triana. They were all capable of hurting others when it came to saving someone you loved.

They moved through the forest quickly, not caring about making a noise. They both dropped to the ground as an intense heat passed over their heads.

"Thanan," Villian whispered, his meaning clear.

Thanan closed everything off. Villian would protect him. He brought the colours together one by one. He could hear nothing but the forming of his mind.

"Very clever. A protection spell. You children have been busy with your trainers. I suspect Barakar will be having a word with Tobias and the others when this is over."

Villian watched closely as the Master came into the clearing. About fifteen children followed. They could barely be older than six. None of them seemed to have creatures, unless they were hiding them as Star had done. He hardened his heart to thoughts of his friend. It was his and Thanan's task to save her and they would not be able to help her if they died, and she would never forgive him in life or death if anything happened to Thanan. Villian found he could stand and the strange glowing light of the protection spell still afforded him a shield from the Master.

"Let the children go. Your time has come to an end," Villian commanded.

The Master threw back his head and laughed. It wasn't a nice sound. Villian looked at Thanan but he was still crouched down, presumably with his eyes closed.

"Barakar asked me to bring one of you back alive. Preferably, Thanan. His magic is stronger than we could have hoped. He will be useful in death. Unlike you."

Villian ducked, even though he trusted Thanan. Lightening shot out of the Master's fingers and crackled around the forcefield. It made his hair stand up, but he felt no pain. Despite the failure, the Master smiled. Villian realised he was testing Thanan's strength.

He tried three more times, each one getting stronger. Villian wondered how much power Thanan and the Master had. Thanan said creating magic drained their energy. He hoped the Master would run out first. Villian looked to the children cowering behind the Master. As he did, he saw an older child coming out of the trees, but the Master was too busy to notice, too confident in his power. The boy whispered to the children, and they all turned to the Master. He'd made a mistake by leaving them behind him, thinking them irrelevant. Villian looked at Thanan, and he could see sweat trickling down his face. He was struggling. He didn't want to alert the Master to the children. He hoped they were here to help them.

As the Master raised his hands to test them again, he arched his back and his hood dropped, revealing a surprisingly young face. A frown aged him, as pain rippled across his face. His mouth opened and a blood-curdling scream made Villian cover his ears. Flames licked at the bottom of his cloak and within moments he was engulfed in flames. Villian couldn't take his eyes off him as the Master fell to the ground and finally fell still. He looked to the children whose faces were pale and a few were crying and holding one another. Today, these poor children had become adults. The older boy nodded at Villian and he whispered to Thanan, "It's okay. You can stop. We are okay. It's safe."

The shimmering forcefield disappeared and Thanan stood up. Villian put an arm on him to steady him. "Are you okay?"

"Yes, I didn't know I could hold it for so long."

"I'm glad you didn't tell me that before."

Thanan grinned. His hair was sticking to his face, sweat still forming on his brow, but he looked alive. His eyes were bright and Prince Villian could swear he saw colours dance in his eyes. Thanan looked down at the burnt form of the Master. "What happened?" he stuttered.

A boy came forward, "I'm Ki." He did sort of a bow at Thanan, who looked wide-eyed at a grinning Villian.

"Ki, I remember you," Thanan said, a blush creeping up his face, which matched the boy's as he said, "You do?" in disbelief.

Thanan looked at Villian again. "Looks like you've become a legend on Luminosa my friend."

"What?" Thanan said stupidly.

The boy came forward, "When you escaped, Galan and Kyla said you would come back and save us. Said you would help us get back to our families. We weren't ready when you arrived. But we are now."

Villian answered, as Thanan had been rendered speechless, his mouth opening and closing without much effect. "Well, it looks like you're the ones saving us. Thank you. All of you."

Villian looked into the tear-streaked faces of the children. They were so small. How had they managed to defeat a Master?

"Do you know where the rest of the children are?"

"Yes. They are in the clearing with the Suckers. I mean dragons. We didn't know." The last words faded.

"Thanan, we must go now. Are you okay?"

Thanan nodded. "I feel a little bit tired but I'm okay."

"Ki, can you lead these children to the cave? Pol is waiting to take you through. You will be safe until we come back."

The boy straightened his back and motioned to the children. They gathered at once around him.

"You will need these," Ki opened his hand. Six red gems sparkled, catching the light which at that moment pushed through the trees.

"They make the magic stronger, which is why we could do this and it doesn't drain your energy as quickly."

"How? Where?" Thanan asked reaching out.

"One of the Masters gave them to us. He told me what to do."

"What?" Villian said. He'd only ever heard bad things about the Masters. Could one of them really be helping them? And why?

Villian and Thanan exchanged a glance. The fact that one of the Masters might be on their side was not something they'd considered. Again, they needed time. Everything happened when they needed to move. They still had to get to Pathanclaw and Pathandon.

"What do I do with them?" Thanan asked, as Ki tipped them into his hand.

"Nothing. He didn't say how they work. He just said to hold them. We all did the fire spell at the same time and it did that." He pointed to the blackened figure on the ground.

Thanan gripped the gems in his hand and felt warmth spread through his body. He felt stronger.

"We must go," Villian said. He reached over and gripped Ki's arm, "Thank you. Get everyone to safety. We will not forget what we have done for us. You should be proud of your bravery."

Ki nodded, unable to speak. Thanan followed Villian's lead and gripped Ki's arm. Villian couldn't hide a smile as all of the children bowed as they passed them. "You're very popular, Thanan. I can see I'm going to have competition for my crown." Thanan blushed a deeper shade of red.

They were quiet as they ran towards danger. They hoped the Masters would be distracted by Pathanclaw and Pathandon. Maybe they could slip in and get the other children away. They realised this was a fool's hope as they made it to the edge of the forest and glanced out of the trees into the strange landscape before them.

The children were lined up in front of the most terrifying sight they had ever seen. Behind them, the female dragons were muzzled as Star's dragon had been. In front, the children were lined up, the ones with creatures far in front of them. One of the Masters had his arm raised, his intent clear. If the dragons attacked, they would kill them. Another Master covered the children. They looked terrified, all of them crying. Thanan doubted any of them would be capable of forming magic. How would they clear their minds enough to protect themselves? He gripped the gems tighter, a rage building as a strange calm descended.

Pol pulled the boat through the cave effortlessly. Looking in Pol frowned at the pale face of their friend. It didn't look like Star, something had gone. Maybe replaced was a better word. Pol pulled Star out of the boat; carried her to the side of the cave and gently laid her head in their lap. Pol smoothed over her blue hair and wiped her face. It was streaked with dust, grime, and sadness. It saddened Pol's heart to think what had been done to the force who was

Star. They knew, Dragon was no longer. Star would never have left Dragon behind.

As Pol stroked her face, Star started to rouse. Her eyelids fluttered as some colour came back into her cheeks. Her breathing became stronger and slowly, her eyes opened. The flaming blue eyes burned into Pol. It was impossible. But here it was, Dragon. The one who Star could never find a name for, was now a part of her.

Chapter 29 – Suntra

Queen Silvarna woke, becoming aware of herself and of her surroundings, aware of another. Her heart leapt. They were both still whole and she had spoken to her heart. He and Pathandon were well. She had detected fear in his voice. Something was about to happen, but they would be joined in a few days. They would be back on Arcus and no longer wondering about the decisions ahead. Their path was clear and she would make it happen. She could see a future for her family.

Rising quickly, she looked to see Bluewing sleeping by her side. Her heart melted at this youngling, grown too soon, with too much responsibility. But soon, she hoped he and her grandson, maybe even her own child would be enjoying their youth once again.

"You are with youngling?"

Queen Silvarna cursed her unguarded mind. She turned to Ember, watching from the dark corner of the cave.

"I would ask you keep this secret for me, Ember. It will not help if this becomes common knowledge. There are tough times ahead and the dragons need my strength."

Ember was silent for a few moments and then nodded, *"I give you my promise, my Queen. But also, I give you hope. You're carrying a female."*

Chapter 30 – Arcus

Lady Cartina held her nerve as two people entered the room, but it took all her effort not to gasp when she heard the unmistakable voices.

"So, you think it is hidden in here somewhere, Baynard?" said the King.

She squeezed her eyes shut and willed herself to be silent. How could they be in here? She pushed her emotions to one side. She might learn something. She had no skills in fighting, planning and wars, but she could listen and help Prince Villian's friends.

"Yes. It has to be. We have searched that dirty, dusty library and found nothing. The same in Raykan's hut before we burnt it down. It has to be hidden somewhere."

"But what if my son has taken it with him?" A fit of coughing overtook the king and it sounded like he'd collapsed heavily into a chair.

"Here, drink some of your mixture. It will help."

The sound of his coughing subsided and Baynard answered his king. "If it cannot be found, then we are lost. We have a little time left to find it before they attack."

Attack! The castle? Her thoughts went to her family, who were in more danger than they knew. She would have to urge them to leave. But how could she tell them why and what she had heard? It must be a book they were speaking of if they had checked the library first.

"You checked Raykan's hut thoroughly? Questioned him?"

"Yes. He's proving stubborn."

"Then make him talk."

"How? You know what he's like. We burnt half his face and body off last time to no effect. He's enchanted."

Lady Cartina felt sick.

"Well, if he won't respond to persuasion, what if we caused someone else pain instead?" the king asked.

Lady Cartina could almost hear Baynard smiling. "Yes, that could work. Do you have any suggestions? We have had no sign of his friends who would be likely to make him open his mouth."

"We know one thing above all else. My son was clearly taken with his betrothed. Maybe Raykan would wish to save his prodigy's young love."

The blood drained from Lady Cartina's body and she felt faint. She squeezed her nails deep into her palms, the pain reviving her. She could not be found. It would mean certain death. The King, Villian's father, was willing to do her harm to get his hands on this book. She had to tell the others, had to escape before they came for her.

Footsteps made her dig her nails in further as one of them stepped towards the window.

"Good idea, my king." She was sure she could smell Baynard's fetid breath. "I will have the guards come in and search the room within the hour. If nothing is found, I will personally see to the task in hand to ensure the maximum discretion."

She couldn't believe they were talking about torturing her to make Raykan talk, to risk the wrath of her father and the sure knowledge of two foes. Who were these people the king needed to find this object for?

"Let us leave. This place reminds me of my first wife. It still has her smell."

Lady Cartina slowly and quietly let out the breath she was holding after they left. Moments later, a tap on the door told her it was safe to leave. She pulled the door open and quickly moved into the corridor. The guard looked white with fear.

"Quick, leave now, my lady. More guards will be back soon."

She touched his arm in thanks and left quickly, not knowing where to go first. To seek out her parents or get a message to Raykan that he needed to escape now, if he hadn't already. Clearly Baynard thought they still had Raykan in chains.

After a few hours, Raykan opened his eyes and stared at the sky. He hadn't realised how much he had missed it after his time locked in the dungeon. He felt rested. He'd conditioned himself not to require much sleep over the years but he wasn't the only one. Valivar was hunched over the fire while Ironhand's snores peppered the quiet night.

Raykan moved with care, his body protesting. He settled himself across from Valivar, who passed him a hot goblet of water. Raykan sprinkled some herbs he'd picked on the way and offered up a few words to enhance the healing effect. He looked up into his old friend's eyes.

"I suppose you have questions, Raykan?"

"One or two, if you don't mind? I won't ask you to break a confidence though."

Valivar nodded and relaxed. He put the book he was reading back into his backpack and raised the goblet to his lips, enjoying the warmth. His fingers always got cold when he lost himself in a book. He stretched out the knots in his back and shoulders and waited.

"Do you think some of the dragons still remain on Arcus?"

After a moment's pause, Valivar replied, "That is some opening question!"

"Well, as we said, the time for secrets is over. I'm sure you can feel it as I can. Things are changing as they haven't in thousands of years. Despite the disappointing news about the prophecy, there is no denying that the portals opened and Prince Villian left. This part of the prophecy came true, even if Prince Villian wasn't the one or there wasn't even one to begin with. Stories often have some truth to them. The magic within me has changed. I feel like someone whose time of death has been announced and the end is coming. I haven't felt my mortality for such a long time. Between us, I feel relief."

Valivar made a noise of agreement, "I too my friend. I've never had your power. I don't have the ability to create your spells and open portals to other worlds. It's been a regret of mine that I've always felt on the cusp of something more. The words I scribed for the dragons were lost to me as I said. I wish I'd negotiated my terms."

Raykan smiled, "And I've always been jealous of you. Magic is a gift and a curse. Our natural inquisitiveness and constant drive to learn and develop mean we are not suited to the wonder that is magic. As soon as I passed the knowledge to my brother, I knew I had done a great wrong. If only we could go back in time."

They were silent, Ironhand's snores mixed with noises of the night creatures.

"Why can't you? The Festival of Time is a clue that the portals can move through time. Can you tell me more about the portals?" Valivar asked. It was good finally to be able to discuss magic and the strange events which had happened so long ago. They both knew Valivar was avoiding Raykan's question.

"You can, no doubt, move to any time, but what right do we have to change the past? There is no telling it would create a better outcome. Maybe those changes would mean we would never have been born, or Villian or Ironhand. Maybe the dragons would have died out naturally. No, I wish I could change it but I would not do it even if given the option. I have done enough."

"You cannot blame yourself forever, my friend. Who would have done anything different in your place? I knew your brother, I knew the power he had over you and everyone else he encountered. He was headstrong and determined from a child, he could manipulate anyone. His destiny was always one of destruction."

Raykan looked up sharply. Despite everything, his instinct was to protect his twin. He sighed as he turned his gaze to the fire.

"I know. I never thought this would happen. That my actions would lead us to the this point and affect so many others. It's weighed too heavy over the years. When Prince Villian was born, I had a feeling something was going to change. That Pathanclaw would also feel the change. Strangely, I was closer to him than my twin, despite being powerless to deny my brother anything."

"What a life. To have been gifted the friendship of a dragon. It makes me shiver every time I think of it. I remember seeing them on the rare occasion they came to Arcus. It was every boy's dream to ride one, and now, what do children dream of?"

Silence settled around them again as they were both lost in dreams of childhood. Valivar filled up their goblets and they waited for the dawn which was starting to show itself on the horizon. The trees began to sparkle with the sunlight and the birds were already awake and searching for food for their hungry chicks. The spring air brought hope.

Ironhand stirred as Valivar added some meat onto the fire, his nose never letting him down. This smith's bones cracked as he stretched. He looked at them both. "What have I missed?"

They both smiled as Ironhand joined them and accepted a drink. Valivar realised it was time to answer Raykan's question and share another secret. But another day was ahead of them. The secrets would save for the evening's fire.

Chapter 31 – Luminosa

Thanan and Villian assessed the sight in front of them. Villian was shocked to see so many dragons. He'd waited his whole life to see one dragon and here he was on a strange planet looking at, not only 'real' dragons, but magical ones. Maybe he hadn't really made it through the portal. Maybe he had died and this was all in his mind. Thanan dug him in the ribs and pointed to the guard.

"If we take him out, I think we can free the dragons," Thanan whispered. "Look at the long metal pins holding the muzzles. Do you think we can pull those out?"

Villian assessed Thanan's plan. Yes, it could work. With the dragons freed they would have the upper hand they needed on the Masters but they needed a distraction.

"Where's Pathandon?"

Thanan looked around, but he couldn't see his friend anywhere. Pathanclaw must have a plan for him to land near the Masters. Thanan didn't know what powers they had but seven against one dragon seemed unfair on the Masters' part. But the Masters knew magic. He hoped Pathanclaw knew what he was doing, however, he smiled thinking of the Master, dead in the woods.

Villian pointed to the girl chained up, "Who is that?"

"It's Kyla. She's really nice, although we never talked that often. She's a bit feisty like Star. She's friends with the one stood in the middle there, Galan. He's the tall one with long hair and the Silver dragon."

"The one missing an arm?"

"Yes, I don't know what happened to him."

Villian marvelled at what these children had been through and how resilient they were to the challenges life had thrown at them. He felt a little ashamed of the privilege he'd had on Arcus and he had thought he had the worst life losing his mother.

"Right, as soon as Pathanclaw gives the signal, I will take out the guard."

Thanan nodded. He felt excited and scared. He looked to Villian, but no doubt his face showed only determination. This was it. It was time to free them all or die trying.

It was hours before Star finally started to rouse again. Pol had pulled the children through which Thanan and Villian had sent. The one named Ki had picked up some food on the way and had settled the children in a dry corner of the cave. They were in awe of the glow worms and soon forgot their peril and started asked questions. Pol had blocked their minds, because they didn't want Star listening to what was going on with the children and the Masters. Star needed to rest. The bright blue eyes had been almost luminescent, like the light from the worms reflected the deep blue pools. Pol wondered if Star knew what had happened.

"Are you okay, Star?" Pol spoke quietly.

Without opening her eyes Star said, "Are you talking again, Pol? That's cool."

Pol smiled.

"Yes, I thought it might be easier."

"How can you do it now, but you couldn't before?"

"Just a touch of magic."

Star smiled, "I feel a bit funny. What's happened?

Where's Dragon? Where are the others? Where are we?"

Pol felt their heart lighten. Star was still in there. Pol sighed. What to say? But Star would only accept the truth.

"Do you remember when we arrived?"

"No. I remember us leaving and then nothing until I woke up here. Well, maybe something, but I'm not sure. I think it was a nightmare."

Pol told Star as gently as they could and held her tight as she sobbed for the loss of her companion. After a while, Star said, "But I feel different, Pol. Something has happened. I don't feel like Dragon has gone."

Pol wasn't sure what to say. It was something they had never thought could happen, that two could mix to become one. But the proof was here, in this wonderful, strong, young human.

"I don't think anyone truly leaves us, Star."

What else could they say? It seemed impossible this child had done the impossible. Her magical creature was now a part of her. Those luminescent eyes were a testament to the endless surprises life could reveal. It never stayed the same.

There were more tears as Star felt the loss, despite her realisation that Dragon hadn't gone. Not completely. She wasn't here. She would never ride alongside the blues, fighting, and protecting the others. What was she going to do now? What was she without Dragon? The tears came again as Pol stroked her hair. Within a few minutes she felt better, lighter, as if Pol's touch were taking away her sadness.

"Are we in the cave where Thanan trained? Is Tobias way up there?" Star pointed to the seemingly endless cave.

"Yes, Tobias is up there. As are all the worms. Once, they travelled the universe. They were the first."

"What do you mean, Pol? They are not from here?"

Pol settled into the story. It was time these humans knew where everything came from and their part in the story as it was. Who knew what Star was becoming? Maybe if she had knowledge of the past, it would help with her future. Maybe they were forging a new future, one which couldn't have been foreseen.

As Pol spoke the other children moved closer. Stories were their link to the outside world. Star smiled at them and beckoned them forward. She knew she should get up and go and fight. Go and help Thanan, Villian, Pathanclaw and Pathandon. But they must be okay, or Pol would have told her otherwise. Her thoughts strayed to Triana. What had become of her? There will still gaps in her memory and she thought maybe she was thankful for that. She felt very tired and closed her eyes as she listened to Pol.

"The worms created the worlds. They were not always fixed here. They moved through time in search of knowledge. They would stay beyond time to watch a planet begin and to die when it couldn't last any longer. Many, many forms came before. Not many survived, not until Arcus. The dragons spent immeasurable time there, until one day, humans were born. The creators watched with interest at how these two great species would survive together. They did for a long time. The dragons never revealed themselves and the humans lived in ignorance of these giant, graceful, kind creatures who lived far away on the same planet. The humans slowly moved further and further out as their numbers grew. But still, they occupied such a small part of their world. The worms finally left. They thought they would be safe and left to settle on Luminosa, knowing, perhaps, their time was ending and it was time to settle before the end. It was on Suntra they finally lost the need to move and settled on Luminosa, it was a very young planet and throughout time, humans were born as were dragons. But they never lasted. Never thrived here. The planet wasn't ready for them.

Star was shocked to hear there had been humans and

dragons here before the Masters had arrived. How could that be? It made her head hurt to think about it as it did when she thought about the Festival of Time and how magic worked. Her mind felt jumbled and eventually she drifted off to sleep again to the gentle strokes on her forehead. Pol's touch, as light as a feather. She'd tried to fight it, she wanted to go and help her friends, but Pol's soothing voice was too much to resist. Soon all the children were asleep and Pol left the ground and found her old friend Tobias.

"It is time," Tobias said.

Chapter 32 – Suntra

Queen Silvarna had found it difficult to keep her mind clear. A female? No females had been born on Suntra. Could this be true? Did they really need to leave this planet? Why now? She needed Pathanclaw's council, the one thing she couldn't get. How could she make this decision on behalf of all dragons when they could stay here? But, maybe Ember was wrong. Maybe it wasn't a female she carried. These thoughts had occupied her mind all the way back from the gem cave.

Bluewing was surprised by the Queen's quiet mind. After she had told him what had passed between her and King Pathanclaw, his heart had soared to know his friend Pathandon was alive and well. He thought they would have been discussing plans, but Queen Silvarna had been distracted when she said they would wait until they returned. Hours later they'd called all the dragons together.

There was a mixture of shock and excitement as General Bluewing announced they would be leaving so soon. The younglings were excited, the Elders worried about a familiar journey. They all knew the trials that lay ahead, but the younglings had no experience of war and death. To see a companion, a friend, die next to you, unable to mourn as they carried on fighting. Bluewing had to settle them all more than once.

The hunters went out to forage. They would have a great feast before they left, not knowing the situation they would find on Arcus. Would it even be as generous as before? They had never wanted for food. Bluewing wanted them all to be fit and ready. The younglings were sent out to practice, if only to keep them occupied while the Elders retired to the cave.

'It is decided then?' General Bluewing looked to each of the Elders, who nodded.

Ember and Aryalax would stay behind with Daysong and Longsong who were needed to channel the power of the gems. If they indeed needed to close the portals after the dragons left, it would be a blow to their powers.

Bluehorn and Kyanite shocked them by stating they would stay behind. They had spoken to their younglings Blueblaze and Blueclaw and decided it was the right thing to do. What if danger arrived on Suntra after they had left? The gem guardians would need more protection. The silver dragons, Firelynx and Arnax added to the sadness by stating they too would stay behind, their three male younglings were nearly grown now and their grandfather, Goch would care for them. General Bluewing was concerned it would reduce their numbers and was surprised Queen Silvarna did not object to their family splitting up. Her silence worried him. But the guardians had said some would need to stay behind to open the portal. Bluewing was grateful he didn't have to decide.

Queen Silvarna couldn't help but feel joy. Could these brave dragons have younglings again? She had thought she would never have a youngling, let alone a female. It was easy to forget the universe was a magical place, full of unknown possibilities. Maybe the time was right. Maybe this was all meant to be. It gave her hope. By keeping her secret she would have the deaths of all who returned from Arcus on her conscience. She wasn't giving them a choice to stay. She had made her peace with her decision. It was the curse of being a leader.

After the council, Bluewing joined the others. He wanted to run through their battle strategy now the others had decided to stay. Queen Silvarna settled into her cave, exhausted by the past few days. She needed to rest, to look after her precious gift. The warmth of the cave and memories of Pathanclaw lulled her to sleep. She hoped they would be reunited in life as well as in her dreams.

Chapter 33 – Arcus

The hall was alive with sounds, but something in the air felt different. A subdued sense of fear and suspense accompanied the evening. Everyone seemed on edge. More and more reports were heard and filtered through the gossiping courtiers. The confused reports about who the attackers were was still unclear to many. Who was in charge of this large unknown army which was reportedly on the move? Who was coming to take the castle and depose the king and their very way of life?

The rumours about Prince Villian were a constant whisper behind fans by the ladies in court as their eyes found Lady Cartina's. Speculation and intrigue were the staple course amongst the privileged. These malicious voices had reached her, and the family knew they were suspected of treachery. Prince Villian had chosen the most inopportune time to leave.

Lady Cartina saw her maid move through the crowd, stopping here and there to share a word and try to dispel the gossiping, whilst picking up whatever snippet of information could be useful to them. Lady Cartina was proud of Lucinda, who was a force as strong as any guard. Her brain was her sword.

As she looked again for her sister, she found her across the room talking to Baynard. Lady Cartina shuddered. How could her sister stand to be near that man? Her skin crawled as she thought about his fetid breath. Her heart still hadn't settled from the experience in Prince Villian's room. As she watched, he lent forward and whispered something in her sister's ear and her sister threw back her head; Lady Cartina was sure no-one else could detect the fake laugh; the quality of her acting could not be argued with. Baynard lent forward again and whispered something for which he received a quite different reaction. Her sister's eyes went wide and she looked around and locked eyes with her sister. The shock in her face soon turned to a mixture of confusion, and then a smile formed, which her sister deemed bode ill for her.

"My Lady, are you okay? You look a little pale." Lucinda was at her Lady's side, her hand holding her arm gently.

"I'm fine. Something is happening tonight. Have you heard anything?"

"I agree, my Lady. No-one seems to..." her voice was cut off to the sounding of the horn, which made some of the ladies squeal and a glass goblet crashed to the floor somewhere. Someone laughed at the mishap. Lady Cartina wished she was like some of these ladies: they really had no idea what was happening.

An excited chatter went about the hall before they were hushed by the royal guard. The royal speaker moved to the front of the raised stone platform where the King and Queen took their meals. The guards stood on the ten long stone steps which separated them from the main hall. Lady Cartina guessed it would be difficult to get to the king, with each step holding a royal guard.

The royal speaker was used to dragging out an announcement, clearly liking to hold the lords and ladies in the palm of his hands. There was silence but for the shuffling of feet, as everyone waited for the news. This is what they lived for. It would be carried back to their houses, the servants attending would trickle it back to the people in the streets, to the harbour and then beyond.

Finally, the speaker reached his news, "My lords and ladies. The King is delighted to announce that the Queen will soon be welcoming a new child. A son will be born. It has been written in the stars."

There was an equal measure of shocked gasps before the loud applause echoed around the room. There were plenty who would benefit if Prince Villian did not take the crown, the ones who didn't believe in the prophecy or the legends of dragons. Lady Cartina felt weak, but clapped along with the rest of the hall. She moved forward as the King and Queen made their way to take their seats. The King looked ill, despite his happiness at the news. She looked at him in a different light after what she had heard in Prince Villian's rooms. The Queen looked much further along in her pregnancy than anyone would have guessed – her seamstress had hidden it well.

The applause and shouts increased as the King held out his hand to his Queen. She looked well and a healthy pink glow touched her cheeks. Lady Cartina imagined the relief she must feel. She'd heard rumours that the king had been looking for a replacement. It seemed very timely that the Queen was finally with child, especially with the heir missing.

The King and Queen took their seats as people queued up to move up the steps and take their turn congratulating the royal couple. Lady Cartina stood behind her mother and father who were the first to offer their wishes and good fortune. But Lady Cartina knew this would worry her father. With a new heir, even if, no, not even, when, she corrected herself, Prince Villian came back and they wed. Would the King let Prince Villian take his place or would he pass it to protectors until the new young prince was of age? How would this leave their family? Not for the first time, Lady Cartina prayed for her prince to return. But he hadn't been gone long and it sounded like Valivar thought it could be months before the prince returned. So much could happen in that time. They needed him to return with the dragons.

"Such a happy occasion. You must be delighted for the King and Queen." Her sister leaned in and whispered in her ear. She could smell the strong wine her sister shouldn't be drinking. She had been warned by their father to stay on her guard.

"It is, my sister. Such a happy occasion. I'm so happy for the queen and Prince Villian will be so happy to learn he has a new brother when he returns."

"Oh, I doubt that, sister."

Lady Cartina refused to take the bait. Helendy was trying to get her to make a show of herself, but she knew her tricks too well.

Her sister sighed, "It seems you've grown up since you became betrothed. It's not at all fun trying to get a rise from you. I will have to take myself elsewhere."

"Yes, please do so."

Helendy laughed. "Oh, I have missed you, my sister. It was so boring back at home without you."

"I doubt that. I'm sure you managed to find someone else to torment. It's a talent you have."

Her sister laughed. It was one of the most frustrating things about her. She never cared whatever anyone said to her. She didn't care about her character, or her faults.

They stopped talking as the guards moved so the family could slowly move up the steps, all eyes on them to see how the King would react. Lady Cartina's father was all congratulations and happiness, her sister certainly could claim her acting skills from him. His congratulations were so earnest that no-one hearing could declare him a liar. The king accepted his congratulations with grace while the Queen blushed at their good wishes.

Later that evening, the Queen's maid sent for Lady Cartina and Lucinda escorted her to the queen's rooms. It was unusual to have a personal audience with the queen.

She had been gentle and welcoming and the first one to check Prince Villian's bride was managing when they learned he'd gone missing.

Lady Cartina felt a knot of anxiety in her stomach as they moved through to the royal quarters. Was this really the king's doing and were they going to take her to the cells to make Raykan talk? Soon after the feast, the queen had left to get her rest to the applause of the hall. The evening had provided an exciting turn of events and Lady Cartina was grateful to leave.

They passed guard after guard as they walked to the queen's quarters. Lady Cartina was sure this wasn't normal. Did they perceive more of a threat now the news had been announced? Or was it the rumours of war? The health of the King had been another whisper. Would he survive to see the baby born? What would happen if he died before Prince Villian was found?

The guards opened the door and Lady Cartina walked tentatively into the room. Lucinda waited on the chair outside the room, feeling intimidated by the two large guards armed with massive swords, who flanked her seat. Lady Cartina twisted her gold ring as she waited. A moment later, the queen's maid beckoned her around the heavy curtained area. She motioned for to her to sit in a chair which had been placed near the bed where the queen now resided, then the maid bowed as she left them. Lady Cartina heard the large doors close. They were alone.

"Good evening, my child. Are you well?" the queen asked with genuine interest.

Lady Cartina always felt it was a shame that this gentle woman was married to such an unlikeable king. But it was a situation she herself might have found herself in with Prince Villian. What if he had been like his father?

"I am very well, my Queen. Thank you for asking, but it should be me asking you. Is there anything I can get you?"

"You are extremely sweet. Maybe you could pass me a drink and please pour one for yourself. It's been a long evening."

Lady Cartina smiled and did as she was bade. The gold goblets were heavy in her hand as she poured the wine from the most exquisite glass jug she had ever seen. She'd heard the king was like a magpie when it came to collecting beautiful pieces. It seemed that included his wives. Prince Villian's mother had been beautiful, as the portrait had testified.

After passing the cup to the queen, she perched on the end of the chair near the queen's bed. Her large skirts were cumbersome but she was an expert and with a quick hand she moved them to the side and smiled.

"How are you, my dear? I'm sure my news is not welcome by all."

Directness was the order of the day. Luckily, Lady Cartina had been skilled in that particular conversation since birth.

"I do not see who would not be happy for you, my Queen. It is joyous news that you will bear a child. I'm sure if Prince Villian were here, he would be overjoyed to have a new brother."

"You talk about my stepson as if you've known him for a lifetime."

Lady Cartina blushed as she thought about the precious few hours she had spent with Prince Villian. Was the queen right? Did she know him at all? His head was full of the great deeds he was about to do. Maybe it had been the excitement in his eyes and she had just been a distraction, a way to appease his father, so he had the alliance with the two great families. Doubt must have shown on her face.

"Oh, child. I am sorry. I can see that my words have distressed you. I assure you it was not my intent. I am merely jealous of your faith and commitment to him after so short a time. I'd given up hope that love at first sight truly existed."

The blush deepened and it wasn't just from the strong wine. She knew some people thought she was only doing her father's bidding. She had been teased by her sister as they grew up when she would always play the princess, falling in love with the prince. Her sister had brought her to tears many times with her laughter and judgement. Now it had happened. It had.

"I know you didn't mean me any ill will, my Queen. I know people think love at first sight is for children and stories. But I'd known Prince Villian a long time before I met him. I'd heard many stories and I didn't believe my hopes and dreams would come true, but they have. Not only that, but I also believe that he will respect me and let me be myself, to achieve my dreams whilst supporting his. I am not my sister but I know what I want and like to get my own way."

The Queen laughed delightedly. "My dear child. You are the match Prince Villian deserves."

She raised a cup and they toasted their hopes and dreams.

"I had hoped, like you, I would marry for love as well as duty. I cannot say I have been as lucky as you. The King is not like his son."

This statement hung in the air like the great bell on the north tower. If the bell rang the castle was in mortal danger, as it would be with these words, if they were heard by another.

"Don't mind me. I think it's the baby making me melancholy. I know I should be the happiest mother in the whole kingdom now. I'm carrying the future king of Arcus. Do you know what this means?"

Lady Cartina knew this meeting was a warning of things to come. The king would clearly favour this new child over Villian. But what could she do about it? She didn't know where he was. Couldn't warn him about what he was coming back to.

"I understand, my queen."

"Do you know where Prince Villian is?"

Lady Cartina shook her head, "No, my queen. He told me he was going on a quest but I know no more than that. I promise."

"I believe you. You have kindness and truth in your heart. If there is any way you can get in touch with him then please tell him to come home before it is too late. Once the baby is born I fear his claim will be dismissed by the council."

"Can I ask..." Lady Cartina broke off. The queen was being very candid with her but she was still the queen.

"Go on, my child. This is a safe place to talk. My walls do not have ears like many in the castle."

"I'm sorry if this sounds rude. But why wouldn't you want your child to rule instead of Villian. I'm not sure I understand."

The Queen sighed, "I am not stupid. I was once, when I was your age and I had dreams of love and happiness in my future. The hope that I could make a difference but, then, here I am." Her hand seemed to take in the whole kingdom as it moved graciously in the air. "I tried to help Villian be the man he is today. He had his mother of course. I met her once, Villian was born in her image, body, mind and soul."

"You are kind, my queen. None can say otherwise."

"It is gracious of you to say but I know what the future holds for my son." She moved one of her gentle hands from her goblet and onto her swollen belly. "I will not have the freedom Villian's mother had. The King has seen what happens and he will not make the same mistake again. My son will be the image of his father and only a shadow of me will remain. If anything at all. I have already lost my unborn son."

Lady Cartina felt a tear spill down her cheek. A sorrow for a mother's son whose destiny was already decided. Her throat felt tight and the words of comfort would not come.

The silence held for a few more moments before the Queen spoke again, "The reason I asked you here was to warn you. You are not a stupid girl and your father will certainly know the ramifications of the birth of my son. It's not only my life in danger but yours as well."

"Why would you be in danger?" Lady Cartina was so startled at this statement she forgot who she was addressing, but the queen didn't seem to notice.

"My child. My unborn son is a danger to many people, as you and Prince Villian are to my child. This baby growing inside me will have blood on its hands before it's even born. How is a child to rise from that? I fear the birth of my child will mean the death of my stepson, Villian, and all those associated with him."

The despair in the queen's voice made Lady Cartina place her goblet on the table and perching on the edge of the bed, she clasped the queen's hand as she composed herself.

"But there is no need for death. Prince Villian and I could be banished. We could run my lands after my father. There is no need for death."

Squeezing her hand, the queen finally let go, and looked into her eyes. Her own eyes were dry now and resolute.

"There is no other choice. You see, the people love Prince Villian and many will not allow him to be expelled from this kingdom. He is their hope for the future for a better Arcus. The King is ill, you know this. Everyone knows this. If his child is born and he dies there will be bloodshed to rule the kingdom. I would not have you and Villian part of this. If Villian does not return soon, I fear you must leave."

A terrible thought passed through Lady Cartina's mind, one she didn't think she was capable of thinking. Her eyes fell on the queen's unborn child and she shuddered.

"It's okay. Your sinful thoughts are not the first to trouble a mind. Now you must go, my child. It will not do well for you to linger too long here. I have loyal guards but Baynard is never far away."

Lady Cartina nodded, it was a lot to take in. She knew the dangers but to have the queen voice them so candidly bode ill. It made her firm in her decision to leave despite them wanting her to stay in the castle. With the threats coming from all sides she had to leave tonight. But first she must warn her family.

Ironhand sat back against the tree rubbing his rock-hard stomach, "Well, that was the best meal I've had in years. I didn't know you could cook so well, Valivar."

"Thank you. Some of us don't live in the ale house and have learned to fend for ourselves."

Ironhand laughed. It was true he ate most of his meals in the tavern. He made their barrels free in exchange for food and ale. He felt he had the better bargain, his appetite was as great as his height. They had been training all day whilst Raykan slept to regain his strength and they were due to leave when dusk fell. Raykan needed to be ready in case they ran into trouble later. Dyana had visited to finalise the plans and give them the worrying news about the announcement of the new child. This put everyone in even more danger, if that were possible.

"I think it is time to finish our conversation," Valivar said abruptly, deciding it could not be put off further.

The others stopped what they were doing when they heard the tone of his voice. Ironhand wiped his large hand across his mouth, "Well, spit it out then. The last few days have felt heavy with untold words. Let's have the rest of them out in the open and be done with it."

Valivar didn't disappoint. "Raykan was right to ask the question yesterday. There are living dragons on Arcus."

Chapter 34 – Luminosa

"**S**o, after all these years, welcome to Suntra, King Pathanclaw You did not give me chance to observe protocol earlier," Barakar bowed.

Pathanclaw felt silence was the best response.

Barakar rose, a smile on his face, "It seems the courtesy of the dragons has waned over the years. But no matter. You are welcome here."

Pathanclaw rose from the ground and flew closer. He circled the dragons, Masters and children before settling to the ground once again. He felt the joy from the other dragons. Pathandon was waiting and the Master would know his grandson was waiting.

"You know why I have come, Barakar. You must release my kin and the children. What you are doing here is barbaric and against the laws of nature. You are teaching humans' magic. That has never ended well."

"Is it? Well, you would know how it ends King Pathanclaw. Without you, this would never be. How does that make you feel? If you hadn't taught my little brother those few skills, none of this would ever have happened. It must hurt your pride, that so many died for your mistake."

Barakar swept his arm to encompass the chained dragons, the terrified children with their abomination of magical creatures. But Pathanclaw had spent months with Star and her magical Dragon. Could he really say Dragon was an abomination? In his heart, he could not. Maybe this was the natural order of things, maybe these were the next evolution. But to what end? Seeing what Barakar had created here only showed the destruction which would be wrought across worlds, if he was allowed to continue. Magic in humans had to stop.

"I'm still paying for my sins, Barakar. I will pay until my last breath. But I will not leave this world in a worse place than when I was born to it. You will return my kin and free the children."

"Will I indeed?" Barakar paced up and down the line, confident in his stride. He knew he had the upper hand. Pathanclaw would not attack the children or endanger his own kin further. It was a stalemate of sorts.

Barakar finally signalled to one of the Masters and they lifted their hands, the signal to the children to lose their magical dragons. A great roar rose into the air from the magical dragons, mixed with cries from the children. The ones who hadn't told their dragons to move were punished swiftly and they soon followed the order. The Master signalled to the man guarding the dragons, and he moved forward with the whip, which the children would feel more than the dragons. They were going nowhere.

It was the chance Villian and Thanan were waiting for. Whilst everyone was distracted, they ran from the forest and hid behind the head of the first dragon. Villian drew his dagger ready to deal with the guard if he needed to. They did not want to risk the Masters seeing them so they had to be quiet and quick.

"Are you ready?" Villian whispered. They were going to try and pull the huge pins from the dragons which they hoped would release their mouths and wings. The giant straps which were covering the dragons' bodies held them to the ground and were attached to the giant iron muzzles. If Villian and Thanan pulled the pins, the huge chain which snaked itself across the dragon's backs, would free them and so they could help King Pathanclaw.

"Yes," Thanan said. He'd been forming the fireball spell in his mind, ready to attack. It was difficult to concentrate on two things and he hoped he could do it. The gems gave him more power and more space in his mind, he could feel something shifting in his mind, gaps opening to allow the magic to flow.

Villian soon realised he wouldn't be able to turn the giant pins with one hand. As he secured his dagger, he daren't risk a look at what was going on. This was the way he could help the children because he knew he was no match against magic. The dragons needed to be free so they could attack the Masters. However, the dragons looked so frail and weak compared to Pathanclaw's great frame, he wondered if they would be strong enough to help.

A voice came into his mind. *"Don't worry about us, Prince Villian, we are ready to stand against our captors. Just set us free."*

Even after all the months of training together it still unsettled Villian to hear a voice in his mind. He could only stand it so long before it gave him terrible head pains. So the others had agreed to talk only this way when necessary. Right now, it was necessary.

"King Pathanclaw, Pathandon. We are ready." He hoped the dragons could hear him.

Villian turned the first giant screw pin. If they were all this hard, it would take forever. Thanan joined him and they got the first three free, but they were sweating and already tiring. They could hear a faint voice, perhaps one of the Masters but they tried to focus on their task. The three pins out on this side, Villian climbed quickly onto the first dragon. The huge clasps were covered in sand and he had to brush it off before finding the strap buckles. He kept his body low and his arms stretched out in front, his hands moving quickly until all the buckles were undone. The heavy chain lay across the top but they were secured by the large metal pins on the floor. He dropped to the other side and helped Thanan to get the others free. They couldn't release the chain until all the pins were out. It would give them away. Villian hoped the dragons would stay still.

"Watch out," Thanan hissed, as he heard one of the guards coming back.

Villian drew his dagger as the guard came closer. He pressed his body again Thanan, shielding him from danger. As the guard moved between the dragon's heads, the dragon turned her head slightly, knocking the guard towards them. With one swift movement Villian slit his throat, caught his body, and dragged it around the back of the dragon, where he hoped he wouldn't be spotted. They waited for a few minutes but they hadn't been discovered and they carried on, the noise beyond shielding their movement.

With a strength he didn't know he had, Thanan pulled the large pin out and, without waiting for his friend, he ran behind the dragon and moved onto the next one as Villian watched, impressed by Thanan's feat. Not to be outdone he put his back into it, swiftly pulling the others out. He climbed up and then over onto another dragon as he released the straps one by one. His hands were bleeding, but he didn't notice. The dragons' movements were restricted but as they moved up the line the dragons tried to position their heads so their rescuers could not be seen so easily, taking care not to loosen the chain.

Meanwhile, Pathanclaw had risen into the air. The magical dragons were coming towards him and he needed to do something.

"Now," shouted Barakar.

"You do not have to do this, Barakar. We can come to terms."

"I doubt it. Attack!"

The nine magical dragons moved as one. The children were frozen to the spot, commanding what felt like a part of them into battle with these giant dragons. They didn't want to do it, but they felt compelled. What would happen if their creatures were killed?

Pathandon flew down silent and fast from the sky. His grandfather had given the signal. As he flew towards the row of Masters, he prepared his fire. Red flame exploded from his mouth, as he aimed carefully so the children would not be harmed. There were screams as the first Master burnt and the shield came down. Pathanclaw was impressed, they needed the protection shield to come down to attack. Pathandon had executed the breaking spell at exactly the right moment as he'd released his fire. From the shocked look on Barakar's face he hadn't realised it was so easy for them to break his shield. He shouldn't have relied on just one Master to provide their shelter. Pathanclaw doubted he would make the same mistake again. He didn't even glance in the direction of Master who was now just a dark patch on the ground.

The magical dragons flew over the burning body and split up, half chasing after Pathandon and the other Pathanclaw. Pathandon wondered why Barakar was allowing this. Did he just want to see the show? Why allow the magical dragons to attack and waste them. They could be no match against them. What was he up to?

Pathandon's powerful wings led the group away. He could stay ahead of them easily. But the further he went, the less help he was to his grandfather. As he'd flown over, he'd spotted Thanan and Villian crawling over the dragons. If they could just free them, the balance of power would be in their favour.

A bolt of pain shot through Pathandon's wing and he realised his mistake. He'd been focused on the magic dragons. As he turned his head, he saw a Master on a magical dragon. It opened its mouth and fire shot in his direction as the other magical dragons closed in.

Pathanclaw rose into the air as the dragons came towards him. They were all smaller than Star's Dragon. He wondered at their power. Star had said it had taken a long time for them to connect and Dragon had grown bigger than any she'd ever seen on Luminosa. It took years to develop powers and by then, the children had usually come of age and been taken away. He heard Pathandon's cry and turned to help him.

Kyla had been working on the gag. Her jaw was aching with the effort, but she had to escape so she could help the others. Galan had looked mortified when he'd had to send his dragon after the one called Pathandon. He couldn't resist the command, no matter how he tried. The heat and scream from the Master had spurred Kyla on. They couldn't be killed, and they didn't have a better chance than now. She had to break free and help. Her eyes were locked straight ahead and she moved her tongue and jaw trying to dislodge the gag, but her mouth was so dry. She saw movement across the top of the dragon in front of her. The dragon turned its head and she could just make out someone crouched on the floor, pulling out the massive pins and someone on top undoing the belts. She had to help them.

Frustratingly she couldn't see anything behind her, but the noises were enough. The ones helping the dragons were almost at the end now. She pulled the threads with her teeth and finally felt the last one give way, and the gag fell to the floor. She moved her tongue trying to get some moisture back. Her knees were aching from being in one position for so long but she put all her pains to one side and concentrated.

Now she could breathe she focused on how to get herself free. She tried to shuffle her hands under her backside. She might not be able to get the clasps off but she would have more freedom of movement and maybe the ones freeing the dragon could help. She closed her eyes and focused trying to ignore the pain in her arms. She had been bound for so long. But she was still alive. There was a movement in the trees and a figure came running towards her. She knew she had been discovered. Her plan to escape was over, she concentrated on a spell. She wouldn't die without a fight.

Chapter 35 – Suntra

I t was time. The ones staying on Suntra had said their goodbyes. They had feasted well and told tales long into the dawn before resting. Now they all waited in the clearing, anticipating their unknown future. Would they ever return? The Guardians said they would close the portal after they left. Would that truly be the end? Queen Silvarna had hope, a desperate hope, but she had hope that maybe some of the dragons could thrive on Suntra and perhaps they would find a way to communicate. Even if they could never visit, maybe the Guardians would somehow find a way.

They all focused on the swirling colours above them. The colours interwove and danced in the air. There had been places on Arcus where the sky radiated colours at certain times of the year, perhaps they were portals of old, no longer capable of joining worlds but never fully leaving no trace.

Queen Silvarna thought of Pathanclaw and Pathandon and willed with all her being that they would return safely to Arcus, hoping the powers that drove them away would have disappeared with time. What if they were still allergic to humans? What if they couldn't turn back? But as Pathanclaw had known it was time, she also knew things had changed. Her unborn was testament to this.

At a signal from Ember, they all rose. Queen Silvarna's eyes sought Ember and the knowledge of their shared secret was reflected in their eyes. The dragons disappeared and the portal closed forever.

Chapter 36 - Arcus

Lady Cartina found her parents in their chamber but her sister was nowhere to be seen. Her mind had been a jumble of thoughts about what to tell them. In the end she told them most of it bar the fact she was leaving and about her new friends.

Her father slammed his hand down on the table, the jug fell off and shattered on the floor. His nostrils flared as he turned on her.

"So, we are in danger are we? I don't need a child to tell me that! As soon as that wretched man spoke of a new child, I knew it spelt disaster. We can only hope the child dies."

"Father!" Lady Cartina shouted.

"Don't be a fool. It's us or that child. I would kill the mother and child myself if I had a chance."

"Lower your voice," her mother hissed.

Her father nodded and kicked at the broken jug.

"What are we to do?"

"There is nothing we can do for now. My men are already on high alert to get us out of here safely if it's needed. Word has been sent for the army to be ready at my command. If we leave now, we risk everything. We have to hope that Prince Villian returns. The people favour him. If only he hadn't left. It has left us all in danger."

"Are you sure you don't know where he is? I've been told that you were with him the morning after the proposal. What did he say?"

So, people were always watching. Not that they had been too careful, since they didn't realise the dangers they already faced. The queen had been pregnant then and the King must have already put his plans in motion. He probably only went ahead with the engagement to secure her family's warriors and get her family here, where the King had control.

"Nothing was said, I've told you before. He said he was going on a quest but didn't tell me where for my own safety."

"Well, that's not gone well. If we knew where he was we might be able to bring him back! Some prince he is, leaving his betrothed to the dangers of this snake pit."

Her father's voice had risen again and it was giving her a headache. There was too much to think about. Her father strode out of the room without saying another word, slamming the door behind him. Her mother came over and hugged her. Lady Cartina nestled into her mother's shoulder, whose long hair smelt of fresh lavender and she felt like a child once more.

Her mother let go and then leaned forward and kissed her forehead. "You're leaving, aren't you?"

Lady Cartina wasn't shocked. Her mother knew her too well.

"Yes. But I'm worried about you and father."

"Not your sister?" Her mother's eyebrow arched.

She smiled, "Maybe a tiny bit."

"Don't worry about us, daughter. The wrath of your father will keep most dangers at bay. His temper can quell most people. But I think it is wise for you to hide until Prince Villian returns and we learn the outcome of the baby's fate. I know it sound barbaric, but this is the world we live in. For now."

Her mother lifted her chin, "You're a strong, kind and I'm sad to say, a very grown-up woman now. I wish I could hold you as I did when you were a child but you have long been an adult, capable of making your own decisions. I trust you always to do the right thing, and sometimes making the right choice means leaving the ones you love behind."

A sob escaped Lady Cartina and she buried her head in her mother's hair one last time, sealing the memory. She broke away first and kissed her mother. After one last look into her eyes, she strode out of the room. It was time to leave.

"Sorry can you say that again?" Ironhand said, pretending to rub his ears.

Despite everything, Valivar smiled, "I said, there are still dragons on Arcus."

"So why in dragons' breath haven't the beasts shown themselves and why have we sent Prince Villian through that bloody portal if there are already dragons here?"

These were valid questions. Valivar looked to Raykan who seemed to have nothing to add to this revelation.

"At the council meeting it was decided that some of the dragons would stay behind. They were sealed into the cave for their protection until the time the others could return safely and free them."

"And how in dragon's teeth do they propose to get them out?"

Valivar passed Ironhand a second batch of bread, hoping a third breakfast might calm his rising temper.

"That I do not know." Before Ironhand could protest he added, "I believe the book I gave Prince Villian holds the key." His hand came up as Ironhand's mouth opened. "Only dragons can break the magical spell. It was no use me keeping the book if we have no dragons. Prince Villian had more chance of convincing the dragons to return if they recognised the text and returned with him to save them."

"That's a lot of ifs!" Ironhand said.

"Actually, it's just one." Valivar counted and was returned with a loud bark of laughter from the smith.

"Well, I don't know what to say. You're quiet, Raykan. I'm sure you have an opinion on the matter."

It was a few more moments before Raykan answered. "I trust, Valivar's decision. Although, since the prophecy is not exactly what we thought, I wonder at your giving away the only thing which could help us free the dragons."

Valivar was a little stung by his tone, "Do you think you could have deciphered the magic and opened it? Don't you think the dragons might be sick of our meddling already?" He paused for a second before adding, "Sorry, Raykan. I should not have spoken to you like that. I let my anger and frustration influence my words. You would think after thousands of years I would have mastered my ability to engage my brain before my mouth. Please accept my apology."

"No apology is needed, my friend. I deserve all the criticism and more." He held his hand out to stop Valivar's protests.

"My heart has been heavier since I learned the truth about the prophecy. I thought nurturing the one would help me atone for my past regrets. I would do anything to set things right and have order and peace once again on Arcus. I have searched my heart and I believe that even though the prophecy is a lie, I saw something in Prince Villian and I felt it in my heart, Pathanclaw and I have always had a link. It's how this all started. I know it was the right path to take. As such, as I know I have done what I think is right, and I believe you have too. Greater forces are at work and we must trust our instincts."

"Are you going to tell us where these dragons are hiding?" Ironhand interrupted.

"Why, are you going to knock on the door with your axe and ask them to come out nicely?" Valivar smiled, as

Ironhand pulled the massive axe from his back in one smooth quick motion.

"Everyone respects the axe!"

"I don't doubt it, especially when it's in your hands, Ironhand."

Ironhand laughed, "What I wouldn't do to get my hands on some dragon fire, gems and good steel. I would create a weapon so great, no enemy could stand in my way."

Valivar raised his eyebrow at Raykan. Ironhand was well known for his skills and love of gems. How his massive shovel hands created the delicate gem encrusted objects, no-one knew. The beauty could cut through the heart as hard as any steel sword his forge produced.

"I think we had better steer clear of anything to do with magic, my friend. Magic is what got us into this after all. We humans are never happy with what we have it seems."

"Well, whilst you all believe in magic and fairy tales some of us have work to do." Ironhand stood up and swung the axe, a smile on his face. This turned to a frown as he heard the explosion in the distance.

"It's time. We will check if it is safe and return to you." With that Valivar and Ironhand moved into the trees leaving Raykan alone. He used the time trying to rest but his mind wouldn't settle. Too much had been revealed. The prophecy being a lie, dragons still alive on Arcus. Everything he'd worked towards for thousands of years was being dismissed. He felt like a youngling. He couldn't help but smile at this. It was their word for the young dragons and it suited them.

He stretched his legs and took the scroll from his backpack. Ironhand had managed to save some of his possessions and he was eternally grateful this was one of them. He unrolled the scroll carefully. Each house had been embellished in iridescent ink. The colours of the dragon houses were strong, even after all these years. His fingers moved over their names, remembering the tales Pathanclaw had told him about his family. He wished he could go back and change things. He sighed. He'd long ago put that idea to rest. It had driven him near mad when the dragons had first left. The prophecy had been the only thing to keep him going throughout the endless years. Had he sent a young boy to his death?

No, no, no. It could not be so. He knew Pathanclaw would be waiting. His old friend would bring Prince Villian back and things would be different. With his last aching bone he would make sure he left this world a better place. He closed his eyes and failed to see or hear the blow. His body crumpled to the ground.

The mist settled on Lady Cartina's cloak, making her shiver. She tightened her arm and brought Lucinda in closer as they moved through the woods. There was a fire blazing on the docks which she thought the captain must have ordered to afford them a distraction to escape. The captain's men had chosen a wooden building which was used to store flammable liquid in pots. The ruse was impressive. The castle had sent a large number of guards to deal with the blaze and the people moved closer to watch the dramatic scene.

She heard a bell toll from the prison. They had discovered Raykan's escape. There was no time to lose.

As soon as she'd heard the explosion, they'd left. Dark clothes had replaced their normal colourful finery and being unused to the weight, the backpack weighed her down. The smog from the fire created eerie shadows amongst the trees. They waited for what felt like an age beside a large oak tree. Finally, they heard the whistle and Ironhand was by their side. Lady Cartina was surprised that he could move so quietly.

He flashed them a big grin and suddenly everything felt okay. They followed him into the woods without question. The quicker they reached the shore the better. They had to get away before anyone noticed. If they were captured, all was lost. Luciana had already updated Dyana that she intended to leave with them. With the news of recent events, they had obviously agreed it was safer for her to leave with them than stay and risk her life in the castle.

They walked for what felt like hours. Lady Cartina was unused to the long walk and every part of her body ached, but she would not slow down or hold anyone up. She could see Ironhand had shortened his great stride to account for them. She was determined they wouldn't be a burden and resolved to work on herself. She needed to learn to defend herself. She would ask Dyana to teach her.

Darkness surrounded them now and the rain beat down harder. They were already soaked to the skin and shivering. The large bags they carried didn't help. The ill-fated weather would help their enemies put out the fires quicker.

Lady Cartina nearly jumped out of her skin and couldn't help but let out a small squeal as a hand covered her mouth. Dyana whispered into her ear and her heart slipped back to where it should be.

"Sorry to startle you, my lady. I will lead you the rest of the way. Ironhand needs to make sure Valivar and Raykan arrive safely."

Lady Cartina nodded and they followed Dyana. She could just make out figures in the trees, and she hoped it was her warriors. The sound of an owl halted their progress, but a few moments later they continued. They must be close, because she could hear the sound of the waves in the distance. She hoped they would continue unmolested but her wish would not be granted. Shadows moved from the forest. Even the animals knew something was coming.

The sound of clashing steal was too loud for the stillness of the woods. They had been discovered. Dyana grabbed her arm, "Stay with Juliana and Jaya. They will get you to the boat."

With that, the warriors were gone and Lady Cartina and Luciana followed swiftly behind the warriors, trying to keep up. The sound of cries and grunts came from all around them, it sounded like a whole army. They came to the top of a steep ridge.

"How will we get down there?" Luciana asked, pointing at the sand, where three small boats were waiting.

"By rope."

Luciana looked wide eyed at the warrior, who seemed nonplussed by the answer, "But, my lady cannot be expected..."

"It's fine, Luciana. We must do as we are told. Come."

Jaya handed Lady Cartina the rope. Lady Cartina thought a look of approval passed her face before being set back into the grim determination the warriors' faces mostly held.

Lady Cartina held the damp rope and took a deep breath, before moving her resisting legs over the edge.

"Hold tight and don't look down. It's not far."

Lady Cartina couldn't reply, she felt terror fill her mind. There was nothing but fresh air below her. She thought of Prince Villian and firmed her resolve. He would not think twice and neither would his warriors. She gritted her teeth and as her feet landed on the sand, she said a prayer as she held the rope and her maid came over the top. The sharp words from Jaya were lost on the wind but whatever she had said made Luciana move quicker down the rope.

Too quickly, her hand slipped and for one terrifying moment, Lady Cartina thought she was going to witness her friend dying in front of her eyes. Her maid had frozen. Jaya came over the top. Could the rope hold them both?

Lady Cartina's neck was hurting as she strained to look up. A few drops of rain preceded a deluge. That was all they needed. Through the rain she could see Jaya had reached Luciana and was guiding her down. Finally, with a cry of gratitude they landed at her feet.

"I'm sorry, my Lady," Luciana said, her teeth with chattering with cold and fear. Gasping for air, her maid hugged her tighter than necessary. "Sorry, my lady. My legs don't seem to want to work."

"It's okay, we are nearly at the boat. Be brave for just a little longer."

A large man came running from one of the boats. Ironhand! Lady Cartina had never been so pleased to see anyone.

"Are you okay?" he said to Luciana. She nodded, but Lady Cartina noticed a bit of colour return to her cheeks when Ironhand touched her shoulder.

Juliana joined them at the bottom making swift work of the rope.

"We must be quick. We met with some resistance. They know we are leaving. We need to move. Dyana and the others have led them away. We will meet them at the next landfall." As she spoke, three more of Villians warriors came over the top of the rope and after touching foreheads with the others ran towards the boat. One of them had blood running down her head but didn't seem to notice. An unusual greeting Lady Cartina thought as she ran.

It was tough going through the sand. Progress was slow for Lady Cartina and her maid who were bone weary by now but trying not to show it. Ironhand took their hands and pulled them forward.

Luciana screamed and fell to the ground. Before Lady Cartina could do anything one of the warriors had taken Ironhand's place and pushed her towards the boat. The warrior was too strong for her to protest. She shouted that she wanted to go back, she thought someone else had been hit. She gasped as her feet met the icy water and very unladylike, the warrior lifted her up and threw her to waiting hands in the boat. She could see Raykan was lying motionless in the bottom.

She turned, not knowing what to do. Ironhand was running with Luciana in his arms, an arrow sticking out of her back. "Noooooo," she cried. Ironhand made it to the boat. As he reached them one of the warriors snapped off part of the arrow, making Luciana scream. She wasn't dead then – Lady Cartina felt relief wash over her. Alive but not out of danger. Ironhand put her in the boat and Lady Cartina shifted so her maid was turned to the side with her head in her lap. She was careful not to move the arrow. Mercifully, Luciana had fainted but was still breathing. Ironhand pushed out the boat with his large frame, grunting at the effort. The man in the boat started rowing as one of the warriors jumped in and helped.

"Where's Jaya?" Juliana asked.

Freya looked up, her eyes filled with tears but her features angry, "She's dead. They shot her too many times. There was nothing I could do."

Tears streamed down Lady Cartina's face. No, it couldn't be. She had just saved their lives only to die as they escaped.

In a flat tone Juliana asked, "Her body? We must go back?"

"We cannot, sister. There are too many. Jaya would not have us risk our lives. You know this."

Lady Cartina stroked her maid's hair. She felt dampness on her leg and ripped off a bit of her skirt and pressed it against the wound. Luciana groaned. The waves were getting bigger and Lady Cartina feared they would be all tipped into the sea. She couldn't swim. To be drowned after all this. The rain lashed them as they finally made it to the ship. Carefully, they moved Raykan and Luciana on board. Lady Cartina looked to the shore. Torch light peppered the land. So many. Her heart went out to Jaya. A brave warrior.

The captain shouted his orders as Ironhand lifted Raykan. Freya and Juliana picked up Luciana.

"Come, my Lady, let's get you all safely into the cabins and then we can make way to pick up the others. This has been a bloody long day."

Lady Cartina thought bloody was right.

Chapter 37 – Luminosa

Triana couldn't cry anymore. She stood, looking again at the empty cages and wondering what she had become. But what could she do? Thanan and Villian wouldn't welcome her after what she had done. The Master had told her to bring Star and Dragon, not to harm them. But she'd become too angry. She didn't know what had come over her. The Masters had shown no interest in her since she returned. She thought they would be grateful for what she had done but she didn't belong anywhere and no-one wanted her. She realised she was being used. The Masters didn't care about her. She had destroyed the talisman so they wouldn't welcome her back. Why hadn't she realised this before? Those months when they had been away, the others had tried to make friends with her and she'd wanted to, but couldn't. They had promised her. Why hadn't she realised. She knew what her worm would say. She was always telling her that she was only a child and shouldn't demand the skills of an adult. But who else did she have? No-one cared about her. Why would they?

She thought the anger would come again but she felt only sadness and emptiness. She opened her hand and looked at the gems. Maybe she could exchange these for her life? Perhaps she could buy her way off Suntra. But where to? She would have to plead with King Pathanclaw. Maybe if she helped them, he would help her escape. She knew things about the Masters which could help the dragons. With one final glance in the empty cages, she stalked out and made her way to the clearing where the Masters had told her to bring Star. It was the place Star had said the Suckers were, or the dragons she had said. Maybe Star had been telling the truth.

Decision made, she ran as fast as she could through the forest. She heard the battle long before she arrived at the clearing where she struggled to take in the sight before her. In front of her, there were dragons lined up! The Suckers! They were telling her the truth, but she'd already known that deep down. In front of the dragons all the children were lined up. The ones with creatures were fixed in a trance on the sky where flames were shooting in all directions. She could just make out the forms of Pathanclaw and Pathandon. The magic dragons were flying through the air, a group of them trying to attack them, but each had their protection spells. Who would tire first and how was the children's magic so strong? Then she heard one of the dragons roar in pain.

She counted quickly. She could only see six Masters. Where were the others? No time for that. A figure was alone crouched on the floor, struggling. Kyla, her friend. Doubts hit her, was she really her friend anymore? Had she ever had been or was she simply scared of her? She looked around but the Masters were busy with the battle. She looked along the line of the chained dragons. A figure on top caught her eye, Villian! They were rescuing the dragons. She had to help. It didn't matter anymore if they trusted her. She had to do something, anything, to help destroy the Masters. But, first, Kyla.

Triana ran low and quickly over to Kyla. Her friend turned, eyes wide in fear. It stung a little but she gritted her teeth and reached her without incident. As she looked up, she spotted a few of the guards were walking towards where she had last seen Thanan. They would be spotted. They had to act quickly.

"Kyla, quick, put your hands as far back as you can."

Kyla didn't even ask what she intended, she'd managed to get her arms under her legs and stretched them out in front, turning her head away. She couldn't help but scream as the searing pain enveloped her wrists. But it wasn't the burning pain she'd expected. She pulled her wrists apart and the metal shackle broke, like ice. Kyla didn't know Triana knew that kind of spell.

Triana crouched low beside her, "Are you okay? We have to go and help Thanan and Villian."

Kyla nodded, wondering why Triana was helping them. Was it a trick? But her old friend seemed genuine. Something had changed in her. A quick look around to make sure they hadn't been seen and Kyla spotted Galan. His face was expressionless, fixed on a point in the sky. She hesitated, wanting to go to him.

"You cannot help him yet. We must get the dragons free. The Masters won't be able to stop them all. Come on." Triana dragged her away.

Villian was drenched in sweat. If the battle hadn't been raging overhead, he wouldn't have been able to see anything. The sky had turned pitch black. Every muscle ached. But there were only two more dragons to go and then they would be able to pull the chains out and free them all. Somehow, maybe the dragons would be able to break them then. He cried out as a white-hot pain flashed across his back. He fell off the side of the dragon and rolled trying to protect himself.

"What the hell do you think you're doing." It was two of the guards. Villian drew his dagger as he rolled away, as the whip cracked the side of the dragon. He needed to get closer. In hand-to-hand battle he would be able to kill them if he had his sword. Thanan was over the other side pulling out the pin. Villian couldn't risk shouting to him. They only had two more pins to release. Thanan would have to carry on. He eyed the guards, as one raised his whip again, about to strike. Villian braced himself for the pain which never came. A scream sounded from the back of the dragon and the guards turned, too late. Two balls of fire ended the guards before they could utter a word.

Triana and a girl he didn't know stood before him. She was as tall as Thanan, with deep brown eyes. "Triana..." he started to say, but she interrupted.

"Look, I know you don't trust me and I've done terrible things. But I promise I'm here to help. We don't have time. We will help you free the dragons."

Villian hesitated. The other girl came forward. "I'm Kyla. My friends are out there and I want to leave this planet, so lets get these dragons free, and kill the Masters."

The girl didn't wait for Villian to answer but ran to one of the pins and started to pull it. Triana joined her and quickly they pulled out the last of the pins.

"I will climb up and do the straps. You look shattered."

Villian didn't get a word in as Kyla climbed the side of the dragon and started undoing the straps. He nodded to Triana. They ran behind the dragon, and caught up with Thanan.

Thanan's eyes widened when he saw Triana, "Thanan we don't have time for this. Pathanclaw, Pathandon and the children need us. Come on."

Kyla slid off the dragon, "Come on. What are you waiting for?"

They rushed into action and soon had all the pins removed and the straps undone. They moved past the last dragon and the four of them tried to pick up the massive chain but it wouldn't budge. Surely they hadn't done all that for nothing.

"What can we do?" Thanan asked, despairing.

"We need to melt the chain," Villain said.

"I know what to do." Triana opened her hand and the gems sparkled in the light of the burning sky, "They make our magic stronger." Triana took Kyla's hand and held out her other to Thanan, a pleading look in her eyes, but she wouldn't beg.

Thanan stepped forward and gripped her hand. They all concentrated and focused on the chain. The flame burnt through the chain and they watched as the black dragon nearest to them finally stood up and shook off the strap holding their wings. The giant metal muzzle crashed to the ground. One by one, along the line, the dragons released themselves from their long imprisonment. They were eager to punish their jailers.

Chapter 38 – Arcus

Valivar made his way back to the camp just as it was turning to dusk, leaving Ironhand to scout further. His body ached, but he felt better for the training. He stopped, listening. The forest was unnaturally silent. He drew his weapons and moved towards the clearing. Raykan was gone. The drag marks showed he had not gone willingly.

"Damn," he said out loud.

Valivar grabbed their belongings, surprised they were still there, wondering why Raykan's captors hadn't taken them. There was nothing else for him here. He moved in the direction of the drag marks., scanning quickly as he moved through towards the coast.

"Lost something?"

He turned sharply, as Dyana came out from behind a tree. He could have sworn he'd checked to the side. Dyana smirked, seeing his glance at the trees behind her.

Two more warriors came through the trees, carrying Raykan's body between them.

"Where did you find him? Is he okay?"

"Scouts from the castle. We have disposed of them. I don't think the captain's diversion has worked as well as we hoped. We must move, and quickly."

Valivar spoke quickly, "Ironhand has gone to scout ahead..."

Dyana cut him off. "We met him. He is going to escort Lady Cartina and Luciana to the ship. It is no longer safe for her in the castle."

Valivar didn't question this turn of events. He nodded and took some of the burden from one of the warriors. They were more skilled than he at tracking. They moved as one through the woods. As they crept closer to the coast a warrior emerged out of the shadows. Dyana gave her swift orders and they blended back into the night. She turned to them.

"I've sent Jaya and Juliana to the meeting point and help Ironhand. They will make sure Lady Cartina and her Luciana get safely to the ship. Freya and Samika, you go to the boat and meet Reena and Gya. Take Valivar and Raykan." The warriors leaned in and touched heads as Jaya and Juliana had done and then they left. Valivar heard Dyana instructing the rest as he followed Reena and Gya.

"The rest with me. Fan out and check the woods. Once everyone is clear, we will meet at the next coastal point."

The warriors blended into the forest as the wind and rain picked up.

They met no resistance as the ship sailed around the coastline, but the weather was becoming too dangerous to get any closer. The captain knew these waters better than anyone. He could not risk the ship.

"We must get out into open sea soon. We will be smashed on the rocks if this continues," Sal shouted.

"There." Juliana pointed to the land.

The captain scanned the coastline and could just make out lights.

"Is it them?" The captain shouted, the howl of the wind nearly drowning out their voices.

"Lower the boats," he cried.

Juliana grabbed the ropes, as another sailor jumped to help. Watching from shore, Valivar thought it was pure madness. They would all be killed, he could barely see anything. How were they to navigate towards the shore?

The others watched, hearts in their mouths as the sailors bravely rowed to shore. A hand on Valivar's back made him turn, "Raykan. You're awake then?"

His friend smiled, "I'm getting a bit sick of getting hit over the head." Valivar's smile deepened, despite the seriousness. Raykan stared out at the scene ahead and gripping tight to Valivar he started to utter words. Valivar felt like every hair on his body rose to the words. Time seemed to stop. The captain crossed himself, the sail dropped as the waves flattened. Someone shouted and Valivar broke away to look to the boat. They had made it to shore and Dyana and the others had made it safely into the boat. They made it quickly back to the boat as the wind and seas fury returned.

"Not bad, my friend." Valivar glanced to Raykan. He managed a thank you before passing out. Valivar caught him and carried him below.

Chapter 39 – Luminosa

Pathanclaw felt pride as he watched Pathandon execute their plans. The Masters' confidence had made them weak. One of them hadn't even protected himself as Pathandon broke through the protection spell, too secure that they had been unbeatable for so long. For all Barakar's powers, he didn't know the old spells. The screams saddened Pathanclaw's heart but gave him hope they could defeat the Master's and save the children and dragons. But were these other Masters doing this with freewill or because of the power Barakar had over them? He concentrated as the other magic dragons came for him. They were no threat, Barakar must know this. Pathanclaw could kill them easily, but he was hoping bloodshed wouldn't be needed as he had no desire to hurt the children, even though they had created these monstrous creatures. Maybe to destroy them would be the best outcome. But how would that affect the children? He did not yet understand how the symbiotic link worked.

Pathanclaw waited as the dragons surrounded him, the air seeming to still as the dragons hovered above him. His eyes had not left Barakar and as he saw the twitch in his left eye, Pathanclaw made up his mind. He was surprised by the power the magical creatures had; the flames would have had as much impact as his if they were full grown. The children could not be capable of such power with their creatures. Star had not had a much time with Dragon and she was more advanced than these. The

Masters were boosting the power and he knew how. Silvarna was right about the gems, somehow Barakar was using their power. He'd already spotted the black spots on the ground. He had already made sense of it but he struggled to acknowledge that Barakar was creating his own gems using the magical power of the children. How could this be? It was an abomination. He knew now this had to stop. He'd been holding the magical dragons back, but now, it had to stop. He could bear the consequences of his actions as he had so often in the past.

Pathandon's cry made him turn sharply to his left and he flew to his grandson's aide. Pathandon had a scorch mark along his side, but he wasn't gravely injured. Pathanclaw signalled to Pathandon, and they circled around until they were high in the air above the magical creatures which had formed together as a pack and were heading towards them. Pathanclaw didn't need to tell his grandson, they could see what they needed to do. They filled their huge lungs and released a devastating rain of fire on the pack. Pathanclaw formed the word in his mind and the flames formed into a ball around them. There would be no escape. Their screams nearly made him falter but it had to be done. Pathandon flew to the side and towards the Masters. He need take no more part in this. Pathanclaw watched as the ball of flames became smaller and smaller, the forcefield he'd created around it shrinking ever closer to the end. His keen ears hurt at the cry of the children below and his heart broke for their loss but he hoped they would understand it was Barakar who had made this come to pass.

Barakar turned as he heard the commotion behind him. It was all going wrong. He'd made an error judging the power of this little group. He would not make the same mistake again. He looked to the sky as the ball of flame consumed the magical dragons. They were of no use to him now and neither were the children. He signalled to the other Masters. It was no matter. They'd didn't need this place anymore. They had had enough. They could have their minor victory. It would give them confidence which would be their undoing, but he wasn't going to leave without a sting in its tail. He smiled.

He kicked at the ash of the Master as he moved into the forest. The children were crying and screaming. The ones who had lost their magical creature were in balls on the floor. Weak. He spotted Triana. So, she thought she could turn to the other side, did she? He signalled to one of the Masters who cast himself in shadows and moved through the chaos as the sand started to swirl in the air, masking their escape.

Kyla came running out from behind the dragons, urging the children to get to safety behind them. She shook Galan, the look on his face would haunt her for the rest of her long days. The newly freed dragons rose into the air, one by one, stiff after countless time shackled to the floor. Some remained to provide shelter for the children. They moved their wings, grateful to feel the air move across their bodies once again. They rose higher and higher into the sky as the sand started to swirl around making it hard for even their keen eyes to focus on the ground below. They couldn't use their wings, it was too dangerous with the children below.

Triana coughed as the small particles swirled around them, the dust making it hard to breathe. They had moved back as the dragons rose into the air. Villian shouted something about getting to the children, to save them but she felt drained despite the power of the gems. Her head hurt so badly, and it was bleeding again, she could feel the trickle of blood down her face and tried to wipe it away. Disorientated, she tried to find the others, but it was useless. She turned, and her scream was stifled as the hand came around her mouth. Words were whispered in her ear and she felt herself relax. She tried to fight the spell, but her body relaxed into the Master's arms. She felt herself being lifted and then knew no more.

"Pathanclaw. Can you do anything? We cannot see." Thanan begged. The children were huddled together but Thanan couldn't see where to take them or where the Masters were.

"Stay where you are. We will come to you."

They felt the ground shake and the sand stopped stinging their faces. Villian risked a look outside of the cloak he had pressed against his face and could see the dragons had created a circle, protecting them with their wings. He heard a scream outside the protection and he sought out Thanan. He'd thought he was next to him.

Pol felt the earth still again and let the children wake. The worst had passed for now. Star wiped her eyes as she woke. The deep sorrow of loss would forever be with her. Pol was sad for that. The world needed people like Star.

"What's happened, Pol? Where are the others? I need to be with them. Need to help."

Pol nodded and told her. It was safe for Star to leave now. The threat had left. She took Star to the boat and one by one sent them on their way. Ki pulled Star through. He had volunteered to guard the tunnel and wait for any others. Star remembered Ki and how nice he'd always been to the other children. His eyes widened as she stared back at him. How bright they now were. He didn't ask about Dragon. He could see it.

Star ran through the forest. She felt like she was outside herself. She felt so much change going on inside but her friends needed her. She couldn't trust Thanan on his own. He would get into all sorts of trouble and Villian couldn't protect him as she could. A sob escaped her as she ran. She couldn't lose Thanan as well as Dragon.

When she finally arrived, it was an unbelievable scene. The first thing she realised was that the dragons were free. They were no longer chained, and it healed her heart just a little bit. Pol would be happy. The dragons took flight as she emerged, and she wondered where they were going. Pathandon had stayed behind to protect the children.

As she scanned them, she realised there were no other creatures, no dragons, no lizards. She knew the children had them, but they were staring sightless, tears had streaking sorrowful paths down their dusty faces. Star could see burnt patches everywhere. She finally found Thanan in the madness before her. He was talking animatedly to Villian. They were alive. She noticed Triana's friend Kyla was there, but it didn't matter. She ran, and as Thanan turned, she rushed into his arms, knocking him to the ground.

"Dragon's teeth. You're even heavier than before. Get off me!" But he laughed and hugged her as they rolled around in the sand, oblivious to the others. Villian held out his hand, pulled Star up and embraced her. She hugged him back fiercely, tears springing to her eyes.

"Thank you," she said, her voice thick with emotion. "Thank you for saving me and looking after Thanan. He needs a lot of looking after."

Villian cleared his throat, "I'm so sorry Star. Sorry, we couldn't save..."

Star pulled back and met his eyes. Villian gasped.

"What is it? "Thanan said, a note of worry back in his voice.

Star turned to him and smiled.

"Star. Your eyes! What?"

"I don't know. I think when, Dragon die..." She couldn't

say it, "I think she's with me. Somehow. I don't know. It's like she hasn't left."

They were all silent. They looked around at the other children whose creatures has perished in the battle, and they hadn't changed in the same way. They had lost something, whereas Star looked more than herself.

"I hope that doesn't mean you're going to be even more annoying!" Thanan said, the lightness of his words not quite matching his tone.

Star punched him on the arm, "Probably worse. And if you think you're going into any more battles without me, you can think again. Look how this went."

Thanan thought they had done well all things considered. The children were free, even if they had lost their creatures. Pathanclaw's kin were free. The Masters were gone, retreating, Pathanclaw had left to deal with them, and they were all still alive. Overall, he thought they had done pretty well.

"I don't know how we managed without you." Thanan said, deciding to agree with her was far less trouble and not being able to stop the massive grin which emerged without bidding.

Star nodded. "Well, don't just stand there grinning like a fool. Fill me in on everything that's happened and let's get these children back to the camp and cleaned up. Honestly, you cannot just stand around here waiting for the Masters to come back and kill us all."

Villian and Thanan grinned stupidly at each other and Villian filled Star in whilst the others encouraged the children to get up. They made a sorry precession as they made their way to the camp.

Star stopped when Villian got to the part about Triana. "She's still alive?" Star's voice was emotionless. It scared Thanan more than her shouting.

"She was, she helped us release the dragons and then the Masters created a sandstorm to escape and Kyla thinks a master took her."

"You were friends with her." Star said it as a statement rather than a question.

Kyla lifted her chin. She wouldn't be intimidated by Star. She felt sorry for her, but it wasn't her fault what Triana had done.

"Star," Thanan said, "It's not Kyla's fault. She helped us."

Star waved her hand. She knew it wasn't. She was glad the Masters had Triana, although she would like to repay the hurt she had done to her and one day, she would. There would be no further forgiveness from her.

"Sorry, Kyla. I know it's not your fault."

Kyla relaxed. She eyed Star in case she changed her mind. With those strange blue eyes of hers she would likely be even more unpredictable.

"Where's Pol?" Thanan asked, only just realising they were not with them.

"Pol stayed in the cave in case we needed them."

Thanan nodded. He felt uneasy for some reason.

They made it to the camp and settled the children. No sooner had they done so, but Pathandon's frantic voice entered their minds.

"Quick, meet us in the oasis. Grandfather has been injured."

They left Ki and Galan in charge of the children and Villian, Thanan, Star and Kyla ran to the oasis. Villian wished he'd had more than a moment to take in the scene before him as breathlessly they reached the oasis. All the female dragons were perched on the surrounding rock faces, looking down. Pathandon was leaning over Pathanclaw.

They ran over. "What's happened?" Villian asked.

"We chased after the Masters. We wanted to stop them escaping but Barakar set a trap. They opened the portal and Pathanclaw tried to close it, but it must have had some

kind of trap on it. I don't know. He was hit with a lightning bolt and fell to the ground. He's alive but he's hurt."

"What can we do? Can Pol heal him?" Prince Villian asked. Pathanclaw was breathing heavily, his eyes shut. A gash in his side was bleeding freely.

"I will go and find Pol," Star said and disappeared before anyone had time to object.

"The Masters have really gone?" Villian asked Pathandon.

"Yes." But Villian detected a lack of conviction. He frowned at Pathandon.

"Not now. Later." Pathandon's familiar voice entered his mind.

Star came running back slightly breathless, "Pol has gone."

"What do you mean, gone?" Thanan questioned.

"I mean, gone. Pol isn't in the cave and I don't know, it's like I cannot feel their presence anymore. Can you feel them?"

Thanan looked around and felt within himself. Star was right. Something was amiss. Missing. He hadn't realised until now. Pol had gone.

"What are we going to do about Pathanclaw?" Star asked.

"He needs time to heal. I think he will be fine. But we need to get to Arcus and soon."

Pathandon filled them in on everything that had happened.

"If we go now, can Pathanclaw follow after?" Prince Villian asked. He was even more desperate to get back. The Masters had gone and it was likely they were returning to Arcus. He needed to return to his home. He had achieved what he had set out to do. Now they would have to rescue his home and his people.

"Yes, with time. Now we have found the others. They can bring him back once he's healed. This place..."

Pathandon trailed off. They all felt the power here.

"I know the words and Prince Villian still has his tattoo. It will direct our path back to Arcus. But we need to go soon. My kin need me."

Pathandon glanced to his grandfather. Could he really go and leave the king here? What if they were trapped or he was too weak to make the journey?

"Can you take us all through?" Villian asked, gesturing to the children and the dragons.

"Yes." He looked up to the other dragons.

Prince Villian thought for a moment and then turned to address the dragons. He sent Kyla back to the camp to speak to the children. They all had a decision to make.

Chapter 40 – Arcus

"**A**re we safe here?" Lady Cartina asked Ironhand. "Yes, my lady."

They had spent terrible long days at sea before the weather had finally settled enough for them to make land.

"Trust me, my lady. No-one will find us here. I've been using this island longer than you've been alive. We have lookouts. Nothing can turn up for miles without one of my men seeing it," Sal said. The captain puffed out his chest, as well he might, the island being like an oasis in the sea.

"Or women," Ironhand said, Prince Villian's warriors had keen eyesight.

"They could show my men a thing or two, that is certain," Sal acknowledged.

"How's Luciana?" Valivar asked, with a wry smile at Ironhand, who blushed. Valivar never failed to reference Luciana when in earshot of the smith and everyone knew it.

"She is wearing her battle scar with honour," Lady Cartina answered. "Her wound will heal in time. She is in no danger now. The herbs Raykan found have healed her wound. She just needs rest."

The captain was a little uneasy. Since the magical spectacle on the boat, most of them had given Raykan a wide berth. They'd heard the rumours about him. It was one thing hearing about it and another to witness it. Sal had seen many a sailor cross himself as he passed the strange old man.

Freya moved amongst the group seated around the fire, passing out salted fish and bread. "What are we going to do now?" Lady Cartina asked, adding her thanks to Freya. The warriors had mourned the loss of Jaya. Guilt pricked at Lady Cartina. If only they had run a bit faster. Dyana had assured her Jaya would have been honoured to die in battle.

"We don't have much of a choice. We lay low here until the signal comes to move," Valivar said.

"And pray, what will the signal be?" the captain asked.

"I have a feeling we will know it when we see it," Ironhand said, looking in the direction of the ship. Raykan had spent days now out of sight.

"Well, I cannot just sit around waiting. I wanted to ask if you would train me to fight?" Lady Cartina looked to Dyana, who looked amused. Lady Cartina picked up the knife she had used to gut the fish earlier. She was determined to make herself useful. She wouldn't be a burden to all of these accomplished people.

Dyana grinned. She picked up her sword, "If you're going to fight, my lady, may I suggest a weapon and not a toothpick."

The chuckle that passed around the camp was welcome. Lady Cartina smiled and took the sword. It was heavier than she thought, and she grunted as the point dropped to the floor. Determined, she picked it up and muscles shaking, lifted it up and settled her face into her best warrior grimace and charged.

A few weeks later a signal went up. Dyana and Lady Cartina ran from the training ground to see what had raised the alarm. They'd heard worrying news from the castle. After Lady Cartina had fled, her father had decided he would bow down no longer. The battle for the kingdom had begun.

"There," the lookout pointed, and they all squinted to the west. A shape moving towards them.

"At last." They turned to see Raykan leaning on his staff. A wide smile transformed his face, so that he looked almost youthful again.

"Is it?" Ironhand said.

"Dragons." Dyana lifted her spear into the air and screamed a battle cry. The answering roar from the distance made every hair stand on end. Lady Cartina turned and hugged Valivar, who returned the gesture without thinking.

"I cannot see..." Ironhand trailed off, "Prince Villian. Can you see?"

They all strained their eyes. A large blue dragon was leading a huge group of dragons, but there was no sign of Prince Villian and a frown began to form on Raykan's face. King Pathanclaw was not amongst them.

"Look." They all turned to Lady Cartina, finding it hard to drag their eyes away from the sight before them. If the dragons were foe, then this would be the last memory they would ever have.

Lady Cartina lifted her hand. The ring was glowing. Swirling colours made it look alive. Raykan took her hand gently and looked into her eyes, "My lady, Prince Villian is coming home."

Thank you for reading my novel, please do consider leaving a review on Amazon or Goodreads. Feedback helps an author to find new readers and we enjoy reading them. Sometimes mistakes are made, an author is only human. If you spot any, give yourself a pat on the back and feel free to message me but please remember us authors can be a sensitive bunch – be nice.

Find out more about me on my website

www.clpeache.com

Other books available on Amazon.

Book Three of the Festival of Time series
is coming soon.

To any writers thinking about self-publishing, go for it, you never know where a bit of courage will take you...

Printed in Great Britain
by Amazon

13381267R00146